The Forbidden Castle

Other books in the U-Ventures series

Return to the Cave of Time
Through the Black Hole

U-VentureS®

The Forbidden Castle

EDWARD PACKARD

Illustrated by DREW WILLIS

SIMON & SCHUSTER BOOKS *for* YOUNG READERS

New York   London   Toronto   Sydney   New Delhi

SIMON & SCHUSTER BOOKS FOR YOUNG READERS
An imprint of Simon & Schuster Children's Publishing Division
1230 Avenue of the Americas, New York, New York 10020
This book is a work of fiction. Any references to historical events, real people, or real places are used fictitiously. Other names, characters, places, and events are products of the author's imagination, and any resemblance to actual events or places or persons, living or dead, is entirely coincidental.
Copyright © 1982, 2013 by Edward Packard
CHOOSE YOUR OWN ADVENTURE is a registered trademark of Chooseco LLC, which is not associated in any manner with this product or U-VENTURES, Edward Packard, Simon & Schuster, Inc., or Expanded Apps, Inc.
U-VENTURES is a registered trademark of Edward Packard.
First Simon & Schuster Books for Young Readers paperback edition April 2013
All rights reserved, including the right of reproduction in whole or in part in any form.
SIMON & SCHUSTER BOOKS FOR YOUNG READERS is a trademark of Simon & Schuster, Inc.
For information about special discounts for bulk purchases, please contact Simon & Schuster Special Sales at 1-866-506-1949 or business@simonandschuster.com.
The Simon & Schuster Speakers Bureau can bring authors to your live event. For more information or to book an event, contact the Simon & Schuster Speakers Bureau at 1-866-248-3049 or visit our website at www.simonspeakers.com.
Book design by Hilary Zarycky
The text for this book is set in ITC Gaillard.
The illustrations for this book are rendered in pen and ink.
Manufactured in the United States of America
0313 OFF
10 9 8 7 6 5 4 3 2 1
Library of Congress Control Number: 2012940290
ISBN 978-1-4424-3428-8
ISBN 978-1-4424-5280-0 (eBook)

FIRST
EDITION

Introduction

You are about to enter a world where kings and nobles rule and wars are fought by knights in armor and soldiers with swords and shields, a world of great stone castles, rich landowners, craftspeople, servants, farmers, monks, nuns, witches, and jesters, a world in which it was hard to tell what was magic and what was real.

It's a dangerous time for you to be alive, but you'll have some advantages. You may meet a witch who will give you a crystal and the power to cast a spell.

There is a chance that you will find half of a secret name that will empower you to reach the Forbidden Castle. Some readers will find the first half of the secret name. Others will find the second half. Once you have found your half, you may be able to find a reader who has found the other half and you can put them together. There is a way to find the other half on your own, but how to do this is something you will have to discover yourself.

Now, on to Europe as it was a thousand years ago. You'll find your way there through the Cave of Time.

Good luck to you!

Edward Packard

It's late in the day when you find the opening behind a boulder in Snake Canyon. The cave seems darker than you remember it, but you step inside, take a second step, and a third, and you slip and are falling down a chute. Your head hits something, but what matters is that here you are, lying in a field, rubbing your scalp and looking up at the branches of an oak tree and the bright blue sky without any idea of where you are.

Around you is mixed pasture and woodland. Nearby is a narrow dirt road, which disappears over a rise a few hundred yards away. Across the road is a fast-flowing stream.

You hear hoofbeats and a strange clanking sound. Someone is coming. You duck behind a clump of bushes. Two men on horseback come over the rise, riding toward you. They are wearing shining metal armor. One of them carries a white shield with a golden lion on it. They must be knights! You watch as they rein in their horses and dismount just a few yards away. They tie their horses to a tree by the stream.

"It has been a long ride, Sir Rupert," says the taller one, "and you've had a long time to think. Have you solved the riddle of the Forbidden Castle?"

"In truth, Sir Godfrey, I have tried, and so has everyone else in England. What a reward King Henry has offered—half the kingdom of Wales!"

"A handsome reward indeed," Sir Godfrey replies, "but not an overgenerous one, for the old monk prophesied that if the king conquered the Forbidden Castle, he would rule all of Europe!"

"He can't conquer the castle unless he can find it!" says Sir Rupert, and the two of them roar with laughter.

Sir Godfrey's face turns serious.

"Even if he solves the riddle, he is not likely to find the Forbidden Castle without the secret name."

"Aye," says Sir Rupert. "And to think I had half of that name and now I can't find it—I thought it was on a piece of paper in my saddlebag."

"You were a dunce not to memorize it," Sir Godfrey says, poking his friend in the arm. "Ah well, it's useless anyway unless you can find out what the missing letters are."

"That's some consolation, I suppose," says Sir Rupert. "The word is eight letters long, and I only had the first four of them."

"Or the last four—we don't even know that,"

says Sir Godfrey. The two knights stroll off out of earshot. You watch them fill their flasks from the stream. As they return to their horses, Sir Godfrey says, "We must get on to Cotwin Castle. King Henry expects us before the sun passes behind the west tower. He will be angry if we are late."

"Aye," says Sir Rupert as he vaults onto his horse. "The king has been in a foul temper since he learned that foreign spies have found their way into the English court. He's ordered that suspicious-looking travelers be locked in the dungeon."

"Aye, and he means it," says Sir Godfrey.

As the two knights prepare to ride off, you wonder whether you should come out from behind your tree. You're wearing twenty-first-century clothing. Surely you will look suspicious to them. On the other hand, you can't stay hidden forever.

Wait for the next passerby, turn to page 4.
Step out from your hiding place, turn to page 12.

The knights ride off and are soon out of sight. On the ground, near where the horses were standing, you spot a scrap of paper.

Turn to either page 8 or page 42.

In a strong voice—one of a man who has made up his mind—the king says, "We shall provide a ship that will take you to France, a half day's voyage from Dover, given a fair wind. There the earl of Kent and three of my best knights shall go with you. Meanwhile, we shall gather our army together—enough men to conquer any castle—and we shall follow as soon as my knights report that you have solved the rest of the riddle and found the castle, maybe sooner! Once we conquer it, all of Europe will be mine!"

He smiles a broad smile, but then his face darkens. Pointing a finger at you, he says, "If you don't find the Forbidden Castle, you will hang from the tallest tree in England!"

Turn to page 44.

You can't believe this is happening! Unless you can think of something brilliant, you're about to die a horrible death!

"May I make a last request?" you ask.

The chancellor looks at you coldly. "What is it?"

"Tell me the riddle of the Forbidden Castle."

"Little good it will do you," he says. "But it is a simple enough request." He steps closer and looks at you curiously. Then he says:

"Somewhere south, where it's colder,
Where that which falls stays where it is,
You'll find what isn't what it is."

You stand there, trying to figure out the riddle. The executioner steps forward with his coil of rope. The guards press you against the stake. A rough, prickly rope pulls tight against your waist. You must say something now!

Say "Give me a little time to solve the riddle,"
turn to page 61.

Say "Stop! I have the solution to the riddle,"
turn to page 166.

"Garth is my name, and you can stay with me, if you like."

"Where do you live?"

He answers with a wave of his arm. "My house is the wide forest! There is plenty of food and plenty to do. It is the only place where a person can be free. Join me if you'd like. Of course, if you are bothered by a little rain and wind and snow now and then, you can follow that road to Cotwin Castle. They'll give you a roof over your head. Though, I must warn you, it might be the roof of a dungeon."

Go with Garth, turn to page 37.
Follow the road to the castle, turn to page 39.

Four letters are scrawled on it: ODYS. You look around, wondering how you can possibly find the other four letters. There's no way of knowing, but you memorize the letters. Then you roll the scrap of paper into a ball and toss it into the bushes.

You are wondering what to do next when you hear a deep voice behind you.

"Are you going to stand there staring at the trees all day?"

Turning, you look up into the eyes of a giant of a man. He is wearing leggings and a tunic made from deerskin. He has a great bushy beard and is holding an ax and a shield.

"You didn't want King Henry's knights to see you, eh?" he says with a laugh and adds, "Then you are a friend to me. Those hayheads give me more trouble than they are worth!" He bends down and looks you over. "What clothes you're wearing! I've never seen the likes of you in these parts!"

"I am a stranger from another place and another time," you say. "Could you tell me what year it is?"

The giant laughs again. "I don't keep track," he says, "and I've never seen why anyone should!

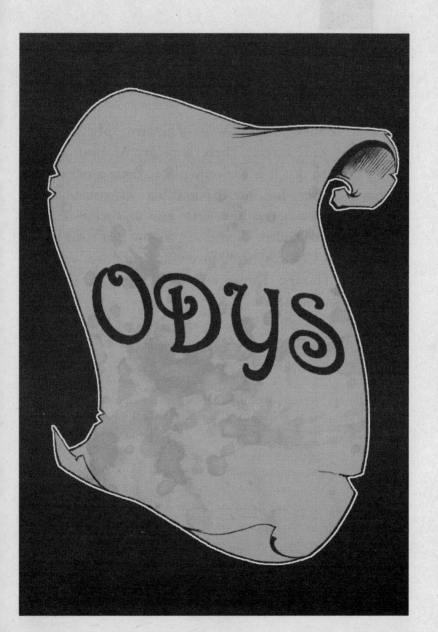

Garth is my name, and you can stay with me, if you like."

"Where do you live?"

He answers with a wave of his arm. "My house is the wide forest! There is plenty of food and plenty to do. It is the only place where a person can be free. Join me if you'd like. Of course, if you are bothered by a little rain and wind and snow now and then, you can follow that road to Cotwin Castle. They'll give you a roof over your head. Though, I must warn you, it might be the roof of a dungeon."

Go with Garth, turn to page 37.
Follow the road to the castle, turn to page 39.

You jump out of the cart, but you're still thinking. Your plan was to run down the road toward the bridge. The woods beyond the bridge should offer you a good hiding place. But what then? Maybe it would be smarter to hide behind the tavern.

Knights of England are not likely popular in France. When they go off looking for you, you might be able to get a French person in the tavern to help you.

Run behind the tavern, turn to page 127.

Try to make it across the bridge and hide in the woods, turn to page 163.

The knights mount their horses. You step out from your hiding place.

"Who are you?" asks Sir Godfrey. "Where did you get those strange garments?"

"I know a spy when I see one," says Sir Rupert. He leans over and roughly pulls you up onto his horse. "If this isn't a spy, it's the devil!"

Sir Godfrey brings his horse alongside. He stares at you intently.

"The devil is crafty and knows how to assume an innocent form, but we shall not be fooled, Rupert! We'll take this one to the castle, and thence to the dungeon."

The knights gallop down the road. You cling to the saddlehorn, trying to keep from falling off, but you can't. Sir Rupert reaches, trying to get hold of you, but loses his grip. You don't know what happens next, because you crack your skull on a rock as you hit the ground.

Sir Godfrey and Sir Rupert gallop on, worrying whether they have been infected by a devil.

The End

You continue on and soon reach a hilltop. It's nearly dark, but there's enough light for you to see a fishing village at the foot of the hill—no more than a dozen houses, each with a little garden—nestled by a harbor, beyond which lies the blue-gray sea.

You feel sure the stranger you talked to was speaking the truth. And you soon learn he was. The first person you meet in the village shows you to the home of Stephen Carter. You knock on the door, introduce yourself, and describe the man you met along the road.

"That's my brother Luke all right," says Carter. "He knows I need someone to help me on my fishing boat. You are dressed in the oddest way I ever saw, but you look like a good sort. Would you like the job? My wife and I could put you up in the boathouse. You'd get an allowance and three meals a day."

You hesitate to answer. You doubt you want to make a career of fishing, but you're tired, hungry, and have nowhere else to go. And there's another good reason for taking the job: You need time to learn the riddle of the Forbidden Castle. You're determined to solve it!

The End

"You called me a devil!" you shout through the hood covering your face. "Only a devil could solve the riddle, and I can do it."

Nothing happens for a moment. You can't tell what's going on because there's still a hood over your head, but you hear voices arguing.

"Stop the execution!" the chancellor says in a loud voice.

Someone pulls off the hood.

"This always happens," the executioner cries. "The prisoner is stalling for time."

"That may be," says the chancellor, "but have you ever seen a prisoner in clothes like these? It's true: A devil may be the one person who can answer the riddle!"

Some of the knights and ladies chant: "No! To the stake! To the stake!"

"Silence!" the chancellor shouts. "King Henry would want to know about this."

Turn to page 166.

You take a few steps into the cave, wondering if a bear might come at you. Michelle goes on a short distance ahead. Suddenly, she cries, "Help, I'm sliding!"

You rush up and grab her arm and try to pull her up, but instead you slip. Then you're falling with her, falling—not, you realize, down a chute in a bear cave, but in the Cave of Time!

Turn to page 115.

You rush out of the cottage and start to hitch the horses to the carriage, but you've hardly begun when they loudly whinny. You pat them and try to calm them, then realize you can't and you'd better make a run for it. Before you even take a step, the baron has his hand on your shoulder.

"Some wizard!" he shouts angrily. "You're nothing but a thief!"

Now the baron is having breakfast with Madame Leeta while you are hanging from your heels, feeling dizzy and hoping they'll have mercy and let you down.

The End

You and Michelle follow Auguste through a forest of towering pines. Late in the day you reach a clear, fast-flowing brook. A fallen tree forms a bridge across it. Beyond the brook are the thickest woods you've ever seen.

"Here I will leave you," Auguste says. "You can camp here for the night. The trail through No Man's Forest begins at the other end of the bridge. If you start out at dawn and travel at a good pace, you will be safely through the forest by sunset. Do not stop to rest. The snakes come out by the time it gets dark. You must lose no time getting through."

You thank Auguste for his help, and camp for the night. Early the next morning you and Michelle cross the bridge and set out on the trail.

Turn to page 20.

Shouting so as to be heard through the hood covering your head, you cry out, "King Henry will be angry if you kill the one person who can solve the riddle!"

You don't know whether anyone hears you. The flames flicker up and your last hope flickers out.

The End

Once you cross the brook, you follow a twisting route that winds around clumps of thorns, plunges into gullies, and goes up steep ridges. Each of you carries a stick to brush aside thorn branches that hang across the path.

You walk briskly without rest. The hours pass. The sun sinks low and the forest grows darker. You keep thinking of the snakes that come out at night. If only you knew how much farther you had to go!

"I am so tired, I can barely walk," says Michelle. "Can we stop for a few moments?"

Agree to rest for a few minutes, turn to page 94.
Insist on continuing on, turn to page 84.

"Let's follow the dragon trail," you tell Michelle.

She nods. "I guess it's as good a bet as any."

You thank Auguste for his help, and start up the narrow winding trail that leads past the Dragon of the Ledges.

The dragon trail turns out to be bordered by thickets and vines and is so narrow that you can only walk single file. You've been hiking about six hours when you stop short. About twenty yards ahead of you and blocking the trail is a large brown bear. You don't think it sees you. It's standing on its hind legs, scooping honey out of a beehive with one paw and swatting away bees with the other.

"What shall we do?" Michelle asks. "There's no way we can get past it."

You get out your magic crystal, thinking of putting a spell on the bear and the bees at the same time! You hold out the crystal. All you have to do now is say the magic word. But maybe you should wait instead.

Try to put a spell on the bear and the bees, turn to page 23.

Wait for the bear to finish eating and go away, turn to page 24.

You hold out the crystal and say the magic word. The bear freezes. The bees that were buzzing about it drop to the ground. You and Michelle hurry past them. "I think we're in the clear," you say.

You continue on for a mile or two more.

Turn to page 26.

You stand there watching the bear. It's getting more and more agitated as it tries to scoop out honey and swat away bees at the same time.

One bee must have gotten through and stung the bear in a sensitive place, because the bear lets out a terrible noise and runs to get away, with the bees chasing it.

The direction the bear runs is right at you and Michelle! You're stung twice by bees before the angry bear gives you a fatal swat with its paw.

The End

Michelle, ahead of you, stops so quickly that you bump into her. Looking ahead, you see a clearing. Scattered about are piles of bones; whether animal or human you cannot tell.

At that moment you hear a hissing sound. A puff of smoke floats toward you. You can tell it came from behind a huge boulder at the far end of the clearing.

Michelle clutches your arm. "The Dragon of the Ledges! It's beyond that big rock!"

"In the twenty-first century, we don't believe in dragons," you say.

"You are not in the twenty-first century!" says Michelle. "Believe me, there are dragons in this century!"

You stay absolutely still. The hissing continues. Puffs of smoke drift toward you. You try to keep from coughing. You wonder whether you can outrun a dragon. You're scared, but you are also curious. You remember that you have the witch's crystal, though you can't be sure it will work on a dragon.

Continue on through the clearing, turn to page 171.

Retreat, turn to page 71.

After breakfast the next morning you and Michelle knock at the chamber of a third Philosopher, Sir René, and find him playing chess with his friend Sir Charles. They listen impatiently while you ask their opinion of Sir Bertram's advice.

"How foolish an argument," says Sir René. "Just because the dragon ran away after the duke blew on his horn does not mean he ran *because* the duke blew on his horn. That is a fallacy. You should ask the stable keeper, who must know about dragons as well as horses."

"Nonsense!" cries Sir Charles. "The stable keeper is a peasant, and therefore would never know the answer. You should go to the estate on the other side of the forest behind the farm. There you will find Count de Rue, a man so worthy that he is often seen in the company of the prince! Not only that, the archbishop says the prince speaks well of him."

"Ah yes, perhaps you are right, Sir Charles," says Sir René. "Count de Rue is a noble man, but you're not right about moving your white bishop to that square." He moves a chess piece across the board and cries, "Checkmate!"

You take Michelle aside. "I think they're all crazy," you whisper. "What do you think?"

"I can't say that they're not," says Michelle. "But they do not seem unkind. One of them might help us find the Forbidden Castle. If only we knew which one to believe . . ."

Journey through the forest to see Count de Rue, turn to page 149.

Talk to yet another Philosopher, turn to page 144.

You look the king in the eye as you speak.

"I thank you humbly for offering me such an honor, Your Majesty, but I wish to find the Forbidden Castle. Would you help me?"

The king shakes a finger at you. "Impudent youth! I am KING! I don't help my subjects. They help me!"

"Well, I can help you. I can win half the kingdom of Wales by finding the Forbidden Castle. Help me a little and I'll help you a lot! I'll give you half of my kingdom."

"Half your kingdom? I'll take half again as much as half," says the king.

"I'll give you half of half again as much as half," you reply.

"Call the royal mathematician," the king says to Stillwell. He looks at you up and down and scowls at you, but then he says:

"You may have wit enough to find the Forbidden Castle. If the royal mathematician approves, we shall leave at sunrise. And by our deeds we proclaim: Rufus shall be king of part of Wales!"

Trumpeters blow their horns, and everyone bows as the king struts out of the royal chamber. You stand there wondering whether the

two of you will find the Forbidden Castle.

You have a feeling you won't, but you should have plenty of laughs along the way.

The End

You bow respectfully and say, "I would be honored to serve in your court, Your Majesty."

"Very well," says the king. "Tonight we shall have a banquet in my honor to welcome you. Stillwell, show our new minister quarters fit for the station to which ministers of such rank are assigned."

"With such enthusiasm as the case warrants," says the jester.

Stillwell leads you up a crumbling stone staircase to a tiny room with stone walls and nothing more than a bed of straw and a hole in the wall for a window.

"Your page will presently attend you," says Stillwell.

You thank him, though your room seems hardly fit for a minister of the king. Your bed is almost as hard as the floor, but you lie down for a nap, for it's been a long time since you've had a good night's sleep.

It seems no more than a minute later when you are awakened by a knock on the door.

"Who is it?"

"A page sent to say that the banquet is about to begin!"

The page leads you down the long spiral stairs

to the great banquet hall. You peer through the archway. Most of the guests are already seated. Your mouth waters at the sight and smell of roast goose, onions, and gravy, but as you start to enter the hall, a great hulk of a man blocks your way.

"You may not enter!" he says.

"But the king himself invited me!"

"The king did not invite you."

"What do you mean?" you ask. "Who are you to contradict me?"

"The Minister of Contradiction!" he replies.

"What kind of title is that?"

"It is my job," he says. "Too many people in this kingdom were contradicting each other, so the king banned it. He has decreed that all contradicting in the kingdom shall be done by me!"

"Is everything you say a contradiction?"

"If you say that, I will contradict it! The king has ordered me to contradict everything that is said by anyone but him."

"Then I cannot come to the banquet!" you say.

"Yes you can!" he shouts.

He steps back a moment, and you dash into the hall and quickly take an empty seat at the grand table. On your left is an old knight with a long, sad face; on your right, a woman wearing a white dress adorned with white lace.

"Who are you?" you ask the woman.

"I am the Lady in Red," she says.

"But your dress is white."

"How dare you contradict me?" she says. "Only the Minister of Contradiction can do that."

Turning to the knight on your left, you ask, "And who are you, sir?"

"The Minister of Laughter," he says with a laugh.

"What does that mean?"

"I decide what is laughable and what is not." He frowns.

You cannot help but laugh.

The minister reddens. "How dare you laugh without my permission?"

At that moment the king stands up and calls for silence. "We welcome a new member of the court." He points at you. "Rise."

You stand up. The king unrolls a long scroll.

"Hmm, we have just appointed a Minister of Craftiness, a Minister of Happiness, a Minister of Inaction, and a Lady of Ladies-in-Waiting. There are only two openings left. Tell us which position you prefer. Would you rather be the Minister of Guesswork or the Minister of Sanity?"

You look around, hardly able to believe what the king has said. King Rufus seems to be even more mad than you'd thought. Silly as it is, you'll have to pick one job or the other.

Say you'll be the Minister of Guesswork, turn to page 145.
Say you'll be the Minister of Sanity, turn to page 141.

"I think we'd better continue on," you tell Michelle. "That cave is just where robbers and bears might be hanging out."

"All right," says Michelle. "The worst that can happen is we'll get wet."

You are soon glad of your decision, for as you walk along, the storm clouds break, the sun begins to shine, and Michelle finds good-tasting nuts. Not only that, you find a place to camp for the night beside a clear, fast-flowing brook.

The next morning, skies are clear, and you set out early.

Turn to page 20.

Garth leads you through the pine forests, across roaring brooks and up steep rock ledges. The sun has dipped below the western hills when you reach a shelter under a rock ledge. You help him gather sticks and pine boughs. The two of you warm your hands in front of a lively fire.

"Why do you live in the woods like this?" you ask.

He grins. "I spread the word that King Henry is no better than anyone else and, ever since, he's had a price on my head. He has lost five of his best knights trying to bring me to the gallows."

"Before I met you, I overheard two knights talking about some riddle. Do you know anything about it?"

"Yes, and it's quite a story. About a year ago an old monk visited the king and told him about a forbidden castle. Of course, the king wanted to know where it was, but the monk wouldn't tell him. Instead, he recited a strange riddle. Then he said, 'Whoever solves the riddle will find the castle. And whoever conquers the castle will rule all of Europe.' Ever since then, the king has been trying to solve the riddle. He's angry because none of his wise men can do it."

"Do you know the answer to the riddle?"

Garth laughs. "I don't even know the riddle. If you want to find out what it is, you must gain admittance to King Henry's court at Cotwin Castle. You may succeed, but if they suspect you of being a spy, they will throw you in the dungeon."

You have no way of knowing what luck you'd have at Cotwin Castle. But it seems risky staying with Garth. He has said himself there's a price on his head.

Go to Cotwin Castle, turn to page 135.
Stay with Garth, turn to page 132.

You thank Garth for his offer, bid him farewell, and set out for Cotwin Castle. You have gone a short distance when you see a woman coming toward you, walking alongside a cart loaded with hay and pulled by a little gray donkey. She is hunched over, almost hidden by her black shawl.

You are hungry and tired. It's getting late in the day. Maybe you should find a place to rest overnight and continue to Cotwin Castle in the morning.

Let the woman pass and continue on to the castle,
turn to page 59.

Ask her where you can get food and shelter for the night,
turn to page 146.

You reach forward, grab the whip from the side of the cart, and take the reins. You crack the whip. The horses lunge forward, knocking the driver to the ground. As the heavy wooden wheels roll past, he scrambles for the side of the cart. You bring the whip down again, shouting, but the driver succeeds in climbing back into the cart. In a moment his burly hand is on your shoulder. With his other hand he grabs the reins and brings the horses to a stop. You are filled with dread as he steers the cart back to the tavern, where the knights are waiting.

"So, my sly friend," says the earl when he sees you. "You would betray the king. There is only one punishment for that, and we shall be quick about carrying it out. Our search for the Forbidden Castle will continue—as soon as you are hanged!"

The End

"Hello," you say. "Could you tell me the riddle of the Forbidden Castle?"

Neither of the guards answer. The taller one unlocks your cell door. They march you up a set of crude stone steps and out into a courtyard. A crowd has gathered. Knights and ladies in colorful clothes are laughing and calling to one another.

In the center of the yard is a pile of wood stacked around a pole. A man stands next to the pole, holding a coil of rope. Another one pulls a hood over your head.

The tall guard leans toward you. "The chancellor will allow a final request before you are tied to the stake." He points to a man, whose dark gray cloak reaches to his ankles.

"Wait!" you cry. "I haven't even had a trial. What am I accused of?"

The chancellor gazes at you with steely gray eyes. "Accused of? Anyone can see by how you're dressed that you're a devil. A trial would be a waste of time."

Turn to page 6.

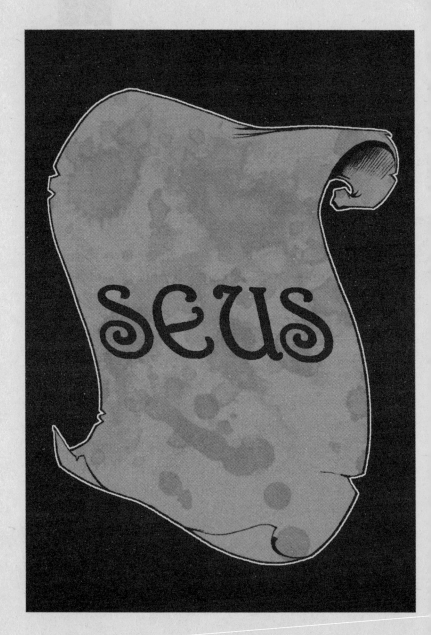

Four letters are scrawled on it: SEUS. You look around, wondering how you can possibly find the other four letters. There's no way of knowing, but you memorize the letters. Then you roll the scrap of paper into a ball and toss it into the bushes.

You are wondering what to do next when you hear a deep voice behind you.

"Are you going to stand there staring at the trees all day?"

Turning, you look up into the eyes of a giant of a man. He is wearing leggings and a tunic made from deerskin. He has a great bushy beard and is holding an ax and a shield.

"You didn't want King Henry's knights to see you, eh?" he says with a laugh and adds, "Then you are a friend to me. Those hayheads give me more trouble than they are worth!" He bends down and looks you over. "What clothes you're wearing! I've never seen the likes of you in these parts!"

"I am a stranger from another place and another time," you say. "Could you tell me what year it is?"

The giant laughs again. "I don't keep track," he says, "and I've never seen why anyone should!"

Turn to page 7.

You shudder a little when you hear this, but you're quick to reply:

"Never fear, Your Majesty. I shall find this castle. Then you shall conquer it, and, as the monk foretold, all Europe shall do homage to your sword!"

"Well spoken," says the king. "Now, make ready, lords, knights, and vassals. Take this wizard in your charge. Brook no delay, and journey all of you to France!"

The trumpets sound, and you are led out of the royal chamber.

Continue to page 45.

You spend half the next day floating down the Thames River on the royal barge. It docks in London. You are eager to see this famous city, although at this time it's a just a little town, but the Earl of Kent has other plans. He swings you up onto his horse and begins riding toward Dover, toward the English Channel. Three knights follow close behind.

The smell of the fresh sea breeze and sight of gulls circling overhead tell you that you have arrived in Dover. One of Henry's ships is tied to a dock, waiting to take you across the channel to France.

You are glad to be safe for the moment, but you keep thinking about what will happen if you can't solve the riddle and find the castle.

That night you board the ship, and men row it out to a mooring a few hundred feet from the dock. The earl tells you that the ship will not set sail till dawn, when the tide will be high.

It's a warm night and you sleep on deck under the watchful eye of one of Henry's knights.

About midnight you wake up and notice that the guard has dozed off. This could be your last chance to escape. But how? There is no moon,

but you can see well enough by the light of the stars. You wonder if you could make it by swimming to shore.

Try to swim to shore, turn to page 48.
Wait for a better chance to escape, turn to page 49.

You slip over the side and slide noiselessly into the water. What a shock! Although it's a warm summer night, the water is much colder than you thought it would be. There's no way you can climb back on to the ship. The sides are too high, and you're weighted down by your wet clothes.

You stroke gamely toward shore, but the cold waters sap your strength, and a strong tide is carrying you down the coast. You don't have the energy to go on. You hold out your crystal, but there is no way you can cast a spell on the cold gray sea.

The End

In the morning you, the Earl of Kent, and three knights set sail. The voyage is a slow one, as your ship has to tack against the wind, but as dawn breaks the next day, you take your first step onto the fertile soil of France.

The earl and his knights mount their powerful horses. They order you to sit in the back of a wooden cart. You soon learn that you are in for a bumpy ride, but the motion lulls you to sleep. You are awakened sometime later by the Earl of Kent calling to the driver.

"Stop here. We shall load our casks with good French wine." Then to you he says, "You stay here. The driver will watch you."

You size up the situation. Your cart has stopped next to a tavern alongside a river. The earl and the knights have gone inside, leaving you alone with the driver. He tilts his head back and closes his eyes. He must be tired from having to drive the horses such a distance with no help from the knights. He looks like he's already asleep! You missed a chance to escape before you sailed to France. Now you have another chance. This time you won't have to swim!

You survey the scene around you. Open pastures lie on both sides of the road. There's no place to hide unless you make it to the bridge that crosses the river a hundred yards or so down the road. Beyond the bridge are thick woods on the far side of the river, where you could hide.

Slip out of the cart and run up the road toward the bridge, turn to page 11.

Seize the reins and urge the horses onward, turn to page 40.

You say, "Oddysus."

The lion roars. It doesn't move, but it looks ready to tear you to pieces if you try to get past it.

"Is there anything you can do to help us?" you ask the old man.

Shaking his head, he replies, "I can guide you to a friendly village where you can live and be comfortable. But until you know the secret name, you can never reach the Forbidden Castle."

The End

You reach the ridge and the end of the trail. Ahead of you, as far as the eye can see, is a mountain wilderness. A chill wind has come up. Snowflakes are fluttering through the air.

"What's this?" the baron cries as he reaches the ridge.

"Nothing!" screams Madame Leeta as she too sees that there is no Forbidden Castle, not even a hut in the desolate landscape ahead.

"You'll pay for this," the baron yells and starts after you. But you are already running back down the trail. They'll never catch you. You're younger and faster than either of them. But you can forget about finding the Forbidden Castle. It will take all your time and energy just to find enough to eat and a place to sleep, and then some way to make a living.

The End

You climb down the tree, moving as silently as you can. Michelle follows. You both stand there awhile, ready to climb back up at any second.

"Let's go," you whisper.

You have almost reached the shallow stream at the edge of the forest when, once again, you hear the howling of the wolves.

Michelle starts to run toward the stream. You follow close behind. But now you see them, at least a dozen gray wolves, running along on either side of you. This time there are no trees to climb. You grab a stick to use as a weapon, but there are too many wolves, and they are hungrier than ever.

The End

After waiting another hour without seeing or hearing any wolves, you climb down the tree, Michelle following closely behind. Keeping a sharp watch, you make your way across the stream and then across a meadow. You climb a steep hill. From the top you can see the mountains beyond. One of them is higher than the others. Patches of snow lie in the gullies near its peak.

"Ah-ha!" you exclaim. "The mountains were closer than we thought. And see the snow? We've gone somewhere south, where it's colder. Maybe we'll see the Forbidden Castle from the top of that mountain."

Continue to page 55.

Late the next day, as you and Michelle wearily climb the steep slope of the mountain, you begin to realize that the distance to the top is much greater than it looked. You doubt whether you can reach the summit. The higher you climb, the colder it gets. The clouds grow thicker and the wind blows harder, bringing fog and rain that ruin your hopes of glimpsing the Forbidden Castle.

Finally, you can climb no farther. You stop—cold, weak, wet, hungry, and exhausted.

Suddenly, you hear a deep, loud barking.

"What's that?" cries Michelle.

"More wolves! Come on! We've got to find shelter!" But even as you are talking, you see two enormous white wolves running toward you. This time, there's no chance you'll escape.

"They're not wolves—they're dogs!" shouts Michelle.

And they are—Great Pyrenees mountain dogs used to guard sheep! One of them jumps up and licks Michelle's face. She laughs. The other tugs at your sleeve. You start playing with it, laughing along with Michelle.

"Michelle, I think they want us to follow them!"

Filled with new energy, you follow the great white dogs over a high ridge. Night will soon be upon you, but the sky grows brighter in the west. The storm clouds are breaking up. By the time you reach the top of the ridge, the mists have lifted. The red sun—about to set—breaks through the clouds.

There, before you, gleaming in the last pink light of the day, is a white stone castle capped by two ivory towers.

You blink and look again. "Michelle, maybe it's the Forbidden Castle!"

"I hope so," Michelle says.

A shepherd comes forth to meet you. The dogs cluster around.

"Tell me, sir," you say, "is this the Forbidden Castle?"

"Just the opposite," he says. "It is the welcoming castle. The lord and lady who own it welcome all strangers as honored guests. I'll show you the way to your quarters. You'll soon be warmed, sitting in front of a well-stoked fire. A fine meal awaits you."

"Thank you, sir," Michelle says, and you add your own thanks.

That night, you lie down on a feather bed, tired but happy, and thinking, if you can't find the Forbidden Castle, this one will do just as well.

The End

You tell the woodsman that you've decided to remain in medieval England awhile. He gives you directions to Cotwin Castle. You thank him and set out on your journey.

You didn't realize it, but bad weather lies ahead. You've gone only a few miles when heavy gray clouds fill the sky. The wind blows harder. The sky darkens. Thunder sounds in the distance, then closer. Lightning flashes across the sky. You start across a broad field. Suddenly, a fierce wind hits you. Sheets of rain pour down. You have no protection, no place to go. You run to the shelter of a big oak tree. Thunder and lightning is everywhere around you.

Suddenly, you remember that you shouldn't seek shelter under a tree in a thunderstorm. You run across a field and throw yourself into a ditch, hoping you won't be a target for a lightning strike. The ditch is full of water. Soaked, you pull yourself up onto the bank, keeping low to minimize your exposure to the lightning. For an hour more you are soaked and chilled by wind and rain, but the storm finally passes. You stand up, shivering from your ordeal, wondering whether you'll survive that night and vowing that, if you ever get home, you'll never go to the Cave of Time again.

The End

"Thanks for the offer," you tell the count. "We would rather have our freedom."

"Very well," he replies. "You are brave, but you are foolish. My lands are beautiful, but robbers, wolves, and bears are no strangers to them."

You start to speak, but the count slaps his horse's side. "Good luck!" he cries, and he and his knights ride briskly away.

You are not sure you made the right decision, but there's nothing to do now but continue through the forest and hope to find food and shelter along the way.

Fortunately, you encounter neither wolves nor robbers, but the weather takes a wild turn. A strong wind blows in from the north, and great dark clouds fill the sky.

Michelle grabs your arm. Pointing, she says, "There's a cave over there. Maybe we should take shelter before the storm hits."

That would seem like a good idea, but you can't help wondering if that cave might be home to a bear.

Tell her it's probably more dangerous to go into the cave than to continue on, turn to page 36.

Agree that it's best to take shelter in the cave, turn to page 16.

After passing the woman with the cart, you follow the road for three or four miles, wondering whether you will ever reach Cotwin Castle or even find food and shelter by nightfall.

The sun is beginning to set when a traveler rides toward you, his cloak billowing behind him. "Where are you headed?" he calls, reining in his horse. You like his warm brown eyes and the friendly expression on his weather-beaten face.

"I'm looking for Cotwin Castle. Am I heading the right way?"

"I'm afraid not," he says. "You missed the road to the left that goes there—it was a half mile back. But it's good for you that you did. If you got there, they would throw you in the dungeon."

"Why?"

"Because of the clothes you are wearing. They would think you are possessed by evil spirits!"

Evil spirits! You are surprised anyone could imagine such a thing. Then you remember that in medieval times evil spirits were often blamed for unusual happenings, and your twenty-first-century clothes are certainly unusual in medieval Europe!

"What am I to do?" you ask.

"Just keep going. You're only a mile or two from a fishing village. When you get there, ask for Stephen Carter. Tell him his brother Luke sent you. You can stay with him and his wife. They will teach you how to catch fish from the sea."

"Are you Luke?" you ask.

"What does it matter?" the stranger says with a grin, and rides off before you can question him more.

Continue on to the fishing village, turn to page 13.
Take your chances at Cotwin Castle, turn to page 62.

"Give me a little time," you say. "I'm sure I can solve the riddle."

The guards laugh.

"Silence!" the chancellor rebukes them, then to you he says, "A little time would do you no good. You couldn't solve it in a hundred years!"

The executioner pulls a hood over your head and finishes tying you to the stake. You're still trying to think of something that could save you.

Say "You called me a devil! Only a devil could solve the riddle!" turn to page 15.

Say "King Henry will be angry if you kill the one person who can solve the riddle," turn to page 19.

What you really want is to find the Forbidden Castle. At least you want a more exciting life than you'll find in a fishing village. You turn and head in the opposite direction, then follow the road the man said would lead to King Henry's castle.

You walk a couple of miles along the road to the castle without seeing anyone. It makes you realize how the population of England a thousand years ago was a tiny fraction of what it will be in the twenty-first century.

By now darkness is setting in, and for all you know, you're still a long way from the castle. You keep going, however, and a little farther on you see a farmhouse. You go up and knock on the door. A woman opens it, takes one look at you, and screams!

"Those clothes you're wearing are the work of the devil," she cries. "They should be burned to a crisp!"

You shrink back when you hear these harsh words.

"Only a devil would be dressed that way!" the man standing behind her shouts. He stands glaring at you, as if ready to hit you if you make a wrong move.

"I'm not a devil," you say. "I'm lost and need shelter for the night."

"Give *you* shelter?" the man shouts. "Be gone with you! Out! Out!"

You run back to the road, then continue on your way. By now it's almost completely dark. You keep walking until you're so tired that you fall asleep by the side of the road.

Sometime later you are awakened by someone roughly handling you. You can't see in the dark, but you can feel what's happening. Whoever has attacked you is taking off your clothes! It must be the man who said you were a devil. His wife said your clothes should be burned!

You struggle as much as you can, but you are no match for your assailant, and in half a minute he has fled, taking your clothes with him!

It's a warm summer night, but you're cold with no clothes on. You get up and start walking down the road just to keep warm.

Summer nights are short in England. It's not long before the sky begins to grow light in the east. You hear a rooster crowing. Soon people will be up and about.

There were mean people in medieval times, just as there are in the twenty-first century, but most people, whatever time they live in, care about the feelings of others. You're sure you'll find someone who will give you clothes to wear, food to eat, and a place to sleep. At least you're no longer in twenty-first-century clothes, so they won't think you're a devil!

The End

Fearing that you could never make it to the Forbidden Castle on your own, you and Michelle agree to stay in the service of the count.

You soon learn that you won't actually be serving the count, but one of his knights. As a page, you must always be ready to assist him. Each day you must prepare his clothing, care for his armor, and wait on his table. You also learn to help him hunt with falcons.

Michelle is in training to be a lady of the court.

Her time is devoted to music, poetry, and Latin, as well as riding. At the end of the day, there is chess and backgammon for you, and astronomy for Michelle. Then bed. Every day is the same. There is plenty of food, and your master is not unkind, but you long to be free.

One day, after you have been in the service of Count Gaston for two months, you and Michelle are summoned to the count's official chamber.

"What's the matter with you two?" the count asks. "You eat well, and you are sheltered from the winds and rain. You have warm clothes. But I get reports that you are both unhappy. Would you rather I had left you to the wolves and bears?"

"No, sire," you say. "It's just that we would

rather be free, and we're eager to get to the Forbidden Castle."

"I understand that," says the count. "But think about this: You are learning skills and about a way of life that you would never have known about before. I think it's a fair arrangement. I will protect you and see that you reach the Forbidden Castle. You have no money to pay me, so you are working instead. It makes perfectly good sense."

"I guess you're right," Michelle says. "I'll try to be more cheerful."

"I can't promise to be more cheerful," you say. "But I agreed to this arrangement, and I'll carry out my end of it."

"Very well," the count says. "Now you may return to your quarters."

Continue to page 67.

"I'm wondering why we thanked him," you say to Michelle as the two of you walk back to your quarters. "He's keeping us prisoner, and he wants us to be cheerful. Thanks for nothing is more like it!"

"The way I look at it," she says, "he is vain and ridiculous, but he's not a bad person. He offered us a deal, and we took it. We said we'd remain in his service for a year, and we've been treated well and are learning a lot of skills. What's the point of irritating him? I'll be polite. It can't do any harm, and it might do some good."

Thinking about it, you decide what Michelle says makes sense.

And so, you and Michelle serve out your year of service, each day wondering if the count will keep his promise to take you to the Forbidden Castle when it ends.

Turn to page 101.

You look the king in the eye.

"I would not bring sorrow. I mean no harm."

Stillwell jumps up and down. "This youth disobeyed Your Highness's command to be silent." The king's face is red with anger.

"For once you make sense, Stillwell. Take this impudent youth to the tower!"

Two guards lay hold of you and drag you out of the courtyard. Outside, they both start laughing.

"No one dares tell the king," one of them says to you, "but the tower steps crumbled away. We have not been able to enter the tower for years!"

The guards laugh so hard that you can't help joining in.

"Then what will happen?" you ask.

"Why, we'll take you to the dungeon," one of the guards says.

"Are you sure?" says the other. "The dungeon stairs have crumbled away too."

Again they both laugh.

"Yes," says the first guard. "But it's easy enough for a prisoner to reach the dungeon without any stairs. Just give a push."

Once again they start laughing, and this time they can't seem to stop. Which is lucky for you.

The drawbridge across the moat is still down. You race across it and head into the woods before anyone thinks to chase you.

As soon as you know you're alone, you start laughing yourself!

The End

"All right," you say to Michelle. "I've always wondered what it's like to be a Gypsy."

An older man places the lute in your hand. You pluck the strings and listen to its rich tones.

"You shall learn to play," says Michelle. "And I shall learn to dance!" She joins the circle of people whirling round the fire to the beat of the tambourine. You begin to pick out a tune on the lute. With each note, the Forbidden Castle and the twenty-first century both seem farther and farther away.

The End

"I don't want our bones lying in that pile," you tell Michelle. "Let's head back the way we came!"

You waste no time hurrying back down the trail, with Michelle right behind you.

For a long time neither of you speaks. It looks as if you've given up your chance to reach the Forbidden Castle.

With a heavy heart you descend the narrow winding trail that leads toward the Philosophers' farm.

The afternoon sun has grown hot when Michelle points to a lake not far from your trail.

"Let's go there to rest and get water," she says.

You cut through the woods to the lake and gratefully sit on a rock and dangle your feet in the cool water. Then you both notice the same thing: a plume of smoke rising from the opposite shore.

"That looks like a campfire," you say. "Maybe we should see who's there. They might be able to guide us to the southern mountains."

As you reach the other side of the lake, Michelle stops short. "Listen! Do you hear the music?"

You slowly creep to the edge of a clearing.

Before you are three brightly painted wagons. It is a Gypsy camp! Horses, dogs, goats, and chickens are scattered about. A dozen or so people are sitting around a fire.

One man shakes a tambourine; another strums a lute. Children are darting in and out of the group. A woman is dishing up steaming stew from a big iron kettle.

Near you, a dark-haired boy, a little older than you, is soothing a colt.

"Whoa, Lightning," he says. "What frightens you?"

The colt turns its head in your direction, sniffing the air. The boy looks, then shouts to the others. In a moment the Gypsies surround you, all of them talking at once.

"Who are you?"

"Where did you come from?"

"Where are you going?"

"We are looking for the Forbidden Castle," says Michelle.

"If it is forbidden," says the boy, "then it cannot be a good thing to find. Why not forget it? Join our band, instead!"

"Yes! Yes!" shout the others.

"But the castle," you begin.

The Gypsy boy takes your wrist and stares at your open palm. "You already have faced great danger. If you continue, far greater danger awaits you." He drops your hand and grins. "If you stay with us, you can ride horses and swim in streams, play music, and have more fun than you would have in any castle."

You look at the spirited horse, and then back at Michelle, who has already put on a crimson scarf. "Let's stay here," she says.

Stay with the Gypsies, turn to page 70.
Continue to search for the Forbidden Castle, turn to page 74.

"The Gypsies are fun to be with," you tell Michelle, "but I don't think I want to live here. I want to find the Forbidden Castle."

"I guess you're right," Michelle says. "Let's rest overnight and leave in the morning."

The Gypsies are sorry to see you go, but they give you food to take with you and show you a path that will guide you safely through the forest. When you ask them about the dragon, they laugh and say that the dragon won't bother you.

You already know the Gypsies well enough to feel sure you can trust them, so you thank them and set out on your way.

Continue to page 75.

Following the Gypsies' instructions, you and Michelle safely make it through the forest. In the months that follow, you search and search, but never find the Forbidden Castle. One day, though, when you least expect it, you find an entrance to the Cave of Time. You decide you have had enough of life a thousand years in the past and you're willing to take your chances on getting back to your own time and your own home.

You're happy when Michelle says she'll come with you.

"I can't promise you what we'll find," you tell her, "but if we get to the twenty-first century, you're going to be *very* surprised by what you see!"

The End

You're afraid to disobey the king by speaking before he does, so you say nothing.

"Well?" the king shouts. "Can't you speak?"

Before you can answer, the jester says, "This youth pretends not to be able to speak, but is clearly dissembling, Your Majesty."

"Dissembling?" the king asks. "That sounds like a crime. Is it?"

"Most assuredly, Your Highness."

"Then what should I do with this malcontent, this reprobate, this . . ."

"'Rat' would be a good word," Stillwell says.

"Exactly, rat!" exclaims the king. "What should be done with this rat?"

"Your Highness, I don't know what not to do."

"Stillwell, only a fool like you would not know what not to do!" says King Rufus. "Why haven't I locked you up in the tower?"

"Because, Your Majesty," says Stillwell, "if you were to lock me up, it would mean you had made a mistake when you appointed me. Since you are perfect, you cannot make a mistake. Therefore, you cannot lock me up."

The king scowls and paces up and down. "We'll talk about this later, Stillwell," he says. Finally, he turns to you.

"You have fallen into my favor," he says.

"It would have been better to have fallen into the moat," says Stillwell.

The king smacks Stillwell on the head with the flat side of his sword. Turning to you he says, "I like your looks. If you agree to serve in my court, I shall make you one of my ministers!"

You realize you've finally had some good luck! The king seems to like you. He's crazy for sure, but maybe he would help you find the Forbidden Castle, though it might be better to wait a while before asking him.

Ask King Rufus to help you find the Forbidden Castle, turn to page 29.

Offer to serve in his court, turn to page 32.

Sir Gregory gives you a box-type trap and some cheese. You have no trouble catching several mice in the barn, and the next morning you and Michelle set out on your journey, carrying your mice with you. Following Sir Gregory's directions, you head for the dragon trail, but there are many forks and branches along the way, and by midafternoon you are totally lost. All you can do is to continue on, hoping to find food and shelter.

Fortunately, you find a tiny cabin with walls of straw and clay. In it, there are two plain cots and a simple chair with a crudely woven rush seat. There is no food in the house except for a few potatoes and roots in a tin box. You're both too cold, hungry, and too tired to cook, so you lie down on the cots to rest.

When you wake up, Michelle is still asleep. A woman dressed in simple peasant clothes is standing over you. You manage to sit up, though you still feel very sleepy. She props a pillow behind you.

"Here, drink this. The English knights are searching for you, but I told them I had not seen anyone who looked like you or your friend. What, may I ask, are you doing here?"

"We are searching for the Forbidden Castle," you say.

"I have heard of it," says the woman. "But I have also heard it exists only in dreams. So you might as well get some more sleep—perhaps you will find it in your dreams!"

You lie back, and quite soon you fall asleep. And you dream of an ivory castle set on a mountain ledge near a waterfall, its tall, rounded towers gleaming in the golden light of the setting sun.

Slowly, you awaken. You open your eyes. The castle is gone, and so is Michelle, and so is the kindly peasant woman. You'll never see either of them again, because, as you can see by looking around, you are back in your own bed, in your own house, in your own time. The strange thing, though, is that there is a box with four mice in it on the floor beside you.

The End

You ask Sir Bertram for his advice.

He laughs. "The truth is that Sir Gregory doesn't know what he's talking about. Just because all elephants are afraid of mice doesn't mean all large animals are afraid of mice! That is called 'a fallacy.' The thing to do is blow on a goat's horn. Then the dragon will leave you alone."

"How do you know this?" you ask.

"How do I know it? Why, it must be so, because the duke of Foully once saw a dragon outside his castle. He leaned out the window and blew on a goat's horn, and the dragon went away!"

Michelle whispers to you, "I have no more idea what to do than before we talked to these men. I'll go with what you decide."

Follow Sir Gregory's advice about taking mice, turn to page 79.

Follow Sir Bertram's advice about taking a goat horn, turn to page 82.

Talk to one of the other Philosophers in the morning, turn to page 27.

Sir Bertram supplies you and Michelle with a goat's horn, shows you how to blow on it properly, and tells you how to find the dragon trail. The next day you set out at dawn, hoping that, by having your goat horn ready, you'll safely get past the dragon and reach the Forbidden Castle.

The trail winds every which way, and you begin to wonder if there's any end to it. You have almost given up hope when you see three knights riding toward you. They rein in their horses.

"You are on the Prince Robert's royal hunting ground!" says one. "You will come with us!"

They lead you and Michelle to a great stone castle set at the crest of the hill. Guards open a gate, and you are marched inside, then down a stone stairway leading to a room below the courtyard. The knights push you inside and lock the door behind you.

The cell you are in is dark and damp. You grope around, but find no place to sleep that night other than piles of hay strewn on the cold stone floor. In the flickering light of a candle burning in the corner you see an enormous rat. Michelle sees it too. You eye it warily. You're afraid that if you go to sleep it will take a piece out of your ear.

"What can we do?" Michelle wonders aloud.

"Tell you what," you say. "I'll stand in the corner and blow the horn. That will get the rat's attention and you can catch it in your pack."

"No," says Michelle. "*I'll* stand over in the corner and blow the horn, and *you* catch it in your pack."

Do as Michelle says, turn to page 152.
Insist on doing it your way, turn to page 154.

"We can't stop now," you say. "It will be dark soon." You hurry along the trail, slowing only to push the thorny branches aside. Deep in the forest, darkness comes quickly. You strain to see each turn in the trail.

"Yikes, a snake!" cries Michelle.

You grab a stick, hook the end of it under the snake, and flip it off to the side.

You both keep moving. Then, Michelle, ahead of you, calls, "It's lighter up ahead!"

A few quick steps and you yell for joy. "Michelle, we made it!" Ahead of you is a field of golden grain. On the hillside beyond it is a stone cottage. A peasant woman is hoeing a small garden. You and Michelle run toward her. She looks up from her work.

"Can you give us some food?" Michelle asks. "We are lost and hungry."

"I would like to help you, but I am a poor serf," says the woman. "I work for the lord of the manor; he is a cruel man. Look, there are two of his knights now!" She points to two men riding toward you.

You're too weary and hungry to try to escape.

"What can we do?" Michelle asks you as the knights rein in their horses and pull to a stop.

You look at her and pat her arm. "We'll see what these knights are like. Just because this woman says the lord of the manor is cruel, it doesn't mean the knights are. Maybe they will help us. If they won't, we'll find others who will."

"Here's what I think," says Michelle. "If we stick together, we'll make it no matter what!"

"And we'll find the Forbidden Castle!" you say as one of the knights dismounts and walks toward you. Your hopes rise as he looks at you with a friendly smile.

The End

"The Forbidden Castle is to the south," you say, "but high in the mountains, where it's colder."

The king stands up and begins to pace around the room, his hands behind his back. Your heart is pounding. Will he praise you or send you to your death?

Suddenly he turns, smiling. "There is wisdom in what you say. I know that in the south of France, there are mountains higher than any in England, and their tops are covered with snow while flowers bloom in the valleys. Now what is the rest of the solution?"

There's no way you can think of what it could be, at least not now.

"Your Majesty," you say. "I am very close to telling you the rest of the answer, but I need time to rest and think. Please grant me until tomorrow morning, and I will tell you then without fail."

The king gives you a long, hard look. "You may be bluffing," he says. "But you have done well so far. I'll give you until tomorrow morning to think of the rest of the answer. Meanwhile . . . Guards, return the prisoner to the dungeon!"

The guards shove you ahead of them down the steep stone stairs and lock you into the same cell you were in before.

You lie in a corner on the cold stone floor, trying to solve the riddle, but you are soon disturbed by a clanking on the door. The guards have arrived with another prisoner. This time it's a wrinkled old woman. She is dressed in rags, and she's so pale that you'd think the blood had been drained from her body. Every bone in her hands is outlined beneath her parched, bleached skin.

She crouches on the floor, stares at you with eyes like a cat's, and croaks out something you can't understand.

She is frightening to look at, but you feel sorry for her. You get a cup from the ledge, fill it with water, and gently hand it to her. She takes it from you and drinks. She tries to speak, but instead starts coughing, like the man whom the guards took away. When she stops, she looks even worse than before.

You offer her more water. She brushes the cup aside. In a hoarse whisper she says, "You are the only person who has ever been kind to me. I give you my only gift." She reaches into an inner pocket of her shawl and withdraws her hand. Between her forefinger and thumb is a yellow-hued crystal no larger than an acorn. She thrusts it at you, and you take it.

"It is a magic crystal," she says. "Use it to cast a spell. Hold it in front of you and say 'Aporia.' But be careful how often you use it. It will work three times and no more."

"Thank you," you say. "What sort of spell are you thinking of?"

She lets out a harsh grating sound and suddenly falls over, face up on the floor, her eyes staring upward. It takes a moment for you to realize that she is dead.

You put the crystal in your pocket and stand staring at her body. You hear the guards returning.

"We only have to tie her to the stake," one says to the other as he unlocks the gate. "The executioner will set the fire."

The guards stare at the shriveled body on the floor.

"Doesn't look like we'll have to tie her," the other guard says.

One of them picks up the poor woman and carries her off, but not before the other points to you. "You'll be next," he says. "First thing in the morning."

He marches off after the other guard.

You know they'll be back. You lie on the

floor trying to decide what to tell them or ask them in the morning, at the same time trying to think of the answer to the rest of the riddle. The mental effort is so great that your body rebels by falling asleep.

The next morning the guards bring you again before the king.

"No more delays," he says. "Answer the next line of the riddle!"

You think of the next line: "Where that which falls stays where it is." Could it have something to do with the setting sun? The sun falls below the horizon yet really stays where it is. But the king is likely to ask what this means. It doesn't exactly solve the riddle.

Say "This has to do with the setting sun, which falls but stays where it is," turn to page 150.

Say "I must go to the southern mountains; then I will be able to tell you," turn to page 92.

"I must go to the southern mountains," you say. "Then I will be able to tell you."

The king frowns, heaves a sigh, and then says, "Very well, but you'd better make sure you do!"

Turn to page 5.

"The Forbidden Castle is to the south," you say, "on the way to the South Pole, where it is cold!"

The king rises, his face reddening with anger. "What nonsense are you telling me? What is this South Pole you speak of?"

Suddenly, you realize the South Pole doesn't mean anything to the king. It won't be reached for almost a thousand years! In the time you're in now, people didn't even know that Earth is round. A flat Earth doesn't have a south pole!

You realize you said the wrong thing and try to think of what to say next, but King Henry roars at his guards. They pick you up like a sack of potatoes and carry you through the door.

"Prepare for execution!" the king calls after them. "And be quick about it!"

The End

"I could use a rest myself," you say, and you sit down on the soft moss beneath a gnarled old tree.

Michelle quickly joins you.

You lean up against the tree and close your eyes. It seems like only a minute later when you open them again, but at least an hour must have gone by, for the sun has set and there is barely enough light to see the trail ahead. Michelle is sound asleep.

"Quick, wake up!" You shake her and pull her to her feet.

The two of you half walk, half run for ten minutes or so before darkness closes in and you are forced to grope your way though the thorns and brambles, barely able to follow the trail. You reach to brush a branch aside, but the branch turns out to be a long slithering snake. It wraps around your arm. It could give you a fatal bite at any moment! With your free hand, you reach into your pocket, take out the crystal, and say the magic word.

The spell worked! The snake drops harmlessly off your arm and lies still on the ground.

"Hurry!" you yell at Michelle. "There are bound to be more."

She's already running ahead. "Open land," she calls back.

In a minute the two of you are out of No Man's Forest. You keep running until you're a quarter of a mile clear of it, and stop to catch your breath.

By now there is not even a glow left in the western sky, but it's a clear mild night, the stars have come out, and the brilliant planet Jupiter hangs high in the south. You camp out for the night.

Although you're worried about wild animals, you're so tired that you quickly fall asleep. In the morning you both wake refreshed and set out early.

Turn to page 26.

You and Michelle quickly reach the stream. It's so cold, it sends shivers up your legs, but you wade easily downstream, for the water hardly rises above your knees. When you're sure you've come far enough so the wolves will lose your scent, you pick your way over round, slippery rocks and walk out on the other side of the stream. Beyond the thin strip of woods ahead of you is a freshly plowed field. You hurry toward it.

You have just reached the field when you hear the pounding of hoofbeats. Three horsemen come over a rise, riding straight for you. Two of them look like common knights, but the third has a dome-shaped helmet topped by a sharp, pointed spike. His face is covered by a full black beard. They rein up beside you.

"Who are you to set foot on the lands of Count Gaston?" the leader demands. You start to explain, but he interrupts. "Have you not heard of me?"

"Are you Count Gaston, sir?"

"I am he. What is your purpose here?"

"We are looking for the Forbidden Castle," Michelle says.

The count laughs. "You are neither wise enough nor strong enough to reach the

Forbidden Castle, for it is high in the mountains to the south. You may travel through my lands on your journey, but I cannot guarantee your safety. If, instead, you agree to remain here in my service, you will live well, and you will learn more than you could by traveling all over Europe. If you stay, know that it shall not be for one day less than a year. But when you have completed your service, my knights and I will guide you to the Forbidden Castle!"

"Can you just tell us how to get there?" you ask.

"I have said what I intended to say," the count replies. "You must make your decision now!"

Michelle takes a long look at you. "This is a tough one. What shall we do?"

Continue on through the lands of Count Gaston, turn to page 58.

Agree to remain in the count's service for not a day less than a year, turn to page 65.

After leaving Madame Leeta you try to retrace your steps to the field where you first found yourself after emerging from the Cave of Time. Following a path through the forest, you come to the hut of a woodsman who gives you food and drink.

"Where are you bound?" he asks.

"I came here from another country and another century through the Cave of Time. I'm trying to find the entrance, so I can return to my own time and my own home. Do you know of it?"

You wonder if the woodsman will laugh at your strange story, but he nods his head and replies, "I'm not surprised to hear this after noticing your strange clothes. You are not the first to visit from another time and place. Well, you're in luck. Since you arrived here, you have walked in a circle. The Cave of Time is almost beneath us. I could show you a tunnel that leads to it."

"I would be most grateful," you say.

"I do not know how grateful you should be," he says. "You might find yourself in a time when the world had turned to fire or to ice!"

You're happy you can get back to the Cave

of Time, but now that you know where it is, you wonder whether it wouldn't be fun to stay in medieval England awhile. You'd still like to solve the riddle and find the Forbidden Castle!

Take the tunnel back into the Cave of Time, turn to page 122.

Stay in medieval England, turn to page 57.

The day the year is up, you and Michelle go to visit the count and demand that he fulfill his half of the bargain.

You sit down in his study, waiting for him.

At last he comes and, with barely a glance at you and Michelle, sits down behind his heavy oak desk.

"I'm glad to see you," he says. "You have both done well and learned a lot in the first year of your service."

"First year!" you say, trying to keep your voice down. "Our one year is up, and it's time for you to keep your promise to guide us to the Forbidden Castle!"

The count pounds the desk as if he's angry, but a smile breaks out on his face. "You didn't listen carefully to my promise," he says. "I said I would guide you to the castle, but you'd first have to serve for not one day less than a year. I didn't say it wouldn't be for more than a year."

"But this isn't fair," Michelle says.

"Oh yes it is," says the count. "It's part of your education, listening carefully to what people say."

"Well, how long will we have to serve then?" you ask.

The count winks at you. Then he says, "You'll have to serve for not one day more than another year. Then my knights and I shall guide you to the Forbidden Castle."

You and Michelle walk dejectedly back to your quarters.

"It's depressing," Michelle says. "But at least this time there's an upper limit on how long we'll have to serve."

"Yeah," you say. "Maybe it will be less than a year."

As it turns out it's only a day. That afternoon the count sends a page to tell you and Michelle to get ready to travel. He and three knights will guide you to the Forbidden Castle in the morning.

The End

"I'm grateful for all you've done for me," you tell Garth. "But I'd like to see more of the world. I'm willing to take my chances with the mad king of Hereford."

"I admire your courage," says Garth. "Rufus may like you, and then again he may not, or he may like you one day and hate you the next. Some say he is generous; some say he is mean. You will soon find out."

For three days Garth travels with you through the forest. When you reach a road that runs alongside a crystal-clear lake, he stops and shakes your hand. "Follow this road for a mile or so, and you will reach Fiddlegate, Rufus's castle. The password is 'gadfly.' Say it three times and they will let you in."

You bid Garth farewell and start along the road. You miss the company of your friend, but you are happy to feel the warm sun on your back and smell the fresh, clean air of the pine forest.

The sun is high overhead when you find yourself at the top of the ridge. Ahead of you is a green valley. Beyond it is a great castle with a stone tower leaning slightly to one side. As you approach the front entrance, you notice that some of the walls are crumbling and the drawbridge is

down. You would think the castle deserted were it not for smoke rising from the courtyard and the cows grazing in a nearby field.

You stand before the drawbridge, wondering whether to cross it. A bugle blows. Two guards appear at the entrance.

"Gadfly, gadfly, gadfly," you say.

The guards look at each other, nod, and, without another word, lead you across the bridge to the large, sunlit courtyard. The yard is covered with broken slate tiles. Clumps of weeds and shrubs poke out of the ground.

Again, the bugle sounds. More guards appear. They surround you and march you through the central arch. They open ranks to let through a short fat man. He wears a blue velvet robe and a golden crown on his head. Behind him is a thin man wearing a pointed cap and bells. Surely this must be King Rufus and his court jester!

A guard steps forward and announces, "King Rufus has deigned to look at you."

You bow. "King Rufus," you say. "I am honored to visit your court."

"Silence! I did not ask you to speak!" says the king. Turning to the jester, he says, "Stillwell, what say you of this intrusion into our royal midst?"

"'Tis a sour sorrow, to us all and all us two," says Stillwell. The king chuckles to himself, then scowls and says nothing.

A guard points a crooked finger at your face. "What have you to say for yourself?"

You feel you should say something, but maybe it would be wiser to wait until the king himself asks a question.

Say something, turn to page 68.
Remain silent, turn to page 77.

"Let us wait for the Philosophers to return," you say. Michelle agrees.

When you tell Auguste that you do not wish to go to No Man's Forest, he shakes his head.

"Well," he says, "I cannot blame you, for the path I would have shown you is a dangerous one. The truth is, in this country and in these times, whatever you do, the odds are against you."

For the next two days you and Michelle help Auguste feed the chickens and milk the goats. At dusk you take one of the dogs and bring the sheep in from the pasture. It's good to have a break in your travels, but you can't stop thinking about the Forbidden Castle. You ask Auguste what he knows about it. He shudders.

"Terrible things have happened there. It is best you do not ask."

You are glad when you finally see the Philosophers riding up the road. They are a scraggly looking lot—of all ages and manner of dress—but they introduce themselves politely and thank you earnestly for helping Auguste take care of the farm.

That evening you sit down to a dinner of mutton and beans. The food is good, but the Philosophers pay no attention to you or Michelle.

Instead, they spend the whole meal arguing over whether a waterfall makes a noise when there is no one close enough to hear it. After dinner they retire to their chambers, except for Sir Bertram and Sir Gregory.

"Where are you bound?" asks Sir Bertram.

"To the Forbidden Castle," you reply.

Sir Bertram raises his eyebrows. "Then you must take the trail past the Dragon of the Ledges. Am I not right, Sir Gregory?"

"Quite so," Sir Gregory replies. "But do not be alarmed. It is simple enough to scare the dragon away. Catch a few mice, put them in a cage, and let them loose in front of the dragon. Then just keep out of its way when it runs."

"How do you know the dragon will be afraid of mice?" you ask.

"It is simple; just a matter of logic. All elephants are afraid of mice. Elephants are large animals. Therefore, all large animals are afraid of mice. Since dragons are large animals, all dragons must be afraid of mice."

Decide to follow Sir Gregory's advice, turn to page 79.

Decide to ask Sir Bertram for his advice, turn to page 81.

In the years that follow your decision to live in the forest, you become as strong and tough as and as expert at hunting and fishing as Garth is.

Once in a while, King Henry sends a group of knights to try to rid people like you from what he thinks of as his private preserve. His knights are brave and skilled—you wouldn't want to meet them on an open field—but in dense woods, they can't maneuver their horses. They often get lost. When they find an open space, they are likely to find you or Garth, crouched on a rock ledge, warning them to leave or to feel the sting of arrows piercing their armor.

Over the years others join you and Garth. Some of your new friends are serfs who have run away from their masters; others are knights who did not wish to spend their lives fighting for a cruel and greedy king.

By the time you grow up, Garth has grown too old to live the rough life of the forest. You become the leader of the clan. You strike a treaty with King Henry: You promise to protect travelers passing through the forest. In return he gives you and your friends a castle of your own.

It's not the kind of life you expected, but it's probably as good as any you could find—almost a thousand years before you were born.

The End

You climb up the tree, right behind Michelle, and none too soon. Within a couple of minutes the wolves arrive, howling and growling at the base of the tree. You're relieved to be safe for the moment, but you're trapped until the wolves go away. There's nothing to do but wait.

Hours later, darkness has begun to fall, and the wolves are still there. Some of them are napping. One quietly licks his paws. Another howls mournfully while a third wolf sits motionless, staring up at you.

There's nothing you can do but huddle against the cold through the long, dark night.

The early morning light reveals no sign of the wolves, and you are eager to be down from the tree and on your way.

"Shall we continue," asks Michelle, "or wait an hour more to make sure they are gone?"

Say "Let's go now," turn to page 53.
Say "Let's wait awhile," turn to page 54.

You tell Madame Leeta you'll help her find the Forbidden Castle. As if to reward you, she starts cooking dinner, stirring lamb stew in a big kettle on her stove. You're thinking how good it smells when the door swings open and a young man walks in. His face is very pale, as though he had never been out in the sun. Behind him, through the open door, you see a fine carriage and the two horses that draw it.

"Ah, Baron de Sal—you are early," says Madame Leeta.

"Who is this?" you ask.

At the same moment the man is pointing at you. "Who is this?" he asks.

To you, Madame Leeta says, "This is Baron de Sal. The most noble knight in England."

To the man, she says, "This is a young wizard who can help me solve the riddle of the Forbidden Castle."

"A wizard?" the baron inquires. "What makes you think so?"

"Show him the magic object," Madame Leeta tells you.

You hold out your cell phone. The baron bends over and examines it. He brushes his fingers over the smooth screen, then steps back, almost as if he's afraid of it.

"With a magic object like that, you may be a wizard," he says.

"And just the wizard we need with us," Madame Leeta says. "Sit down, baron, there's enough stew for the three of us. You can sleep in the barn tonight. There is a bed above the hayloft, where you will be warm and comfortable."

"I will sleep in the barn," says the baron, "but first let the wizard tell us the answer to the riddle."

You hold up your cell phone and pretend to be studying it. This does nothing to help you solve the riddle, but at least gives you time to think. In a firm voice you say, "Baron, you shall know the first part of the riddle in the morning."

"Very well," says the baron. "But if you can't tell me in the morning, I will assume you are not a wizard but a fraud who should be hung by the heels!"

The baron goes out to attend to his horses.

"The baron has a foul temper," Madame Leeta says once the two of you are alone. "But it doesn't matter. I am sure you'll be able to tell the answer to the riddle by morning."

Turn to page 114.

An hour has passed. You can hear Madame Leeta snoring. The baron went to the barn some time ago. He's probably sleeping soundly, but you're not.

You're trying to solve the riddle and having no luck. You know that if you can't solve it, the baron is going to be very angry with you in the morning. You don't like the way he talked about hanging you by your heels!

Lie in bed and try to solve the riddle, turn to page 117.

Rush out of the cottage and try to make a getaway in the baron's carriage, turn to page 17.

Walk out of the cottage and try to get as far as you can on foot, turn to page 116.

It is broad daylight. You and Michelle are sitting in a field. A two-lane road is only a dozen feet away. A bus goes by. A big tractor-trailer is right behind it. *Whoosh*. An SUV whizzes past.

Michelle screams. "What are those monsters? What a noise! It is horrible!"

"Everything's just fine," you say. You're looking across the road at the familiar sign that makes you wonder what Michelle would think of a hamburger and a shake.

The End

You jump out of bed, get dressed, take what scraps of food you can find, slip out of the cottage, and start down the road. You're eager to get as far from the baron and Madame Leeta as you can before they are up.

By the time you've gone several miles, you're too tired to go any more. You lie down on a bed of pine needles at the edge of the forest. Tired as you are, it takes a while to sleep, for instead of sleeping, you are thinking: *If only I could have solved the riddle, I could have found the Forbidden Castle. If only I could find Garth, I could stay with him in the forest. If only I could find the entrance to the Cave of Time, I could get home again. If only people were kinder a thousand years ago. If only this were a dream . . . and I'm waking up. I'm waking up. What's going on? Someone's calling me . . .*

"Time to get up! You'll be late for school!"

The End

You keep trying to think of the answer to the riddle, trying not to fall asleep. It's not long before you're sound asleep anyway. When you wake up, it's already light outside. Soon the others will be up, and you haven't even begun to solve the riddle! You sit up in bed, trying to think more clearly. You run the first line of the riddle over in your head: "Somewhere south, where it's colder . . ."

Normally it will be warmer, not cooler, if you go south. Mountains might be cooler, even if they are farther south, and you remember that there are mountains in part of southern France—the Alps.

There's a knock on the door, which opens before you can answer.

"I see you're up early." It's Madame Leeta. "Here's Baron de Sal," she adds as the baron looks in.

"Good morning," you say sleepily.

"It will be a good morning if you tell us the answer to the riddle," says the baron.

You don't know the answer to the whole riddle, but you may know the answer to the first part, so you say, "My magic object tells me that the castle is in southern France, in the mountains known as the Alps. We must journey there. Then I shall be able to answer the rest of the riddle."

The baron and Madame Leeta exchange glances.

"Very well," says the baron. "We shall go to the mountains in southern France, but I warn you: If you don't solve the riddle when we get there, you shall hang by your heels until the vultures make a meal of you!"

Continue to page 119.

Riding with Baron de Sal and Madame Leeta in the baron's carriage, you journey to Dover, where the baron hires a boatman to take you to France.

After a rough channel crossing and a week's travel across the French countryside, you, Madame Leeta, and the baron reach the top of a high hill in southern France. The baron stops the carriage. The high peaks of the Alps lie before you.

"So," the baron says to you, "we have come all this distance. Are you sure the Forbidden Castle is in these mountains?"

"Of course!" Madame Leeta answers for you. "That's the only explanation for the first line of the riddle—'Somewhere south, where it is colder.' If you go south, it gets warmer, unless you go into the mountains!" She glares at you and points. "There are the mountains, but I see no castle! You must tell us the solution to the second line of the riddle—'Where that which falls stays where it is.'"

"It's time for you to use your magic object," says the baron.

You glance at your cell phone and tap it, pretending it might tell you something. If only it could work!

"Well?" says the baron in an angry voice.

Should you admit that you can't solve the riddle, or should you bluff and tell them you will solve it soon?

Admit you can't solve the riddle, continue to page 121.
Tell them you'll solve the riddle soon, turn to page 174.

"I don't think I can solve the rest of the riddle," you say.

"Fraud! Wasting our time and money!" the baron cries. He lunges at you, but you are already out of the carriage, running down the road, then cutting across a steep grassy slope. The baron is after you, screaming. You look back over your shoulder and see him trip on a rock and fall to the ground. In a moment he is up again and limping after you, but you know he can't catch you now.

You continue down the mountain and follow the sound of church bells until you reach a tiny village in the valley below. There you find refuge with a kind couple who offer you food and shelter in exchange for your promise to tend their sheep and goats.

So it is that you begin a new life in the mountains of southern France. The work is pleasant and the scenery is beautiful, but you know you won't be happy until you find the Forbidden Castle. You're determined to keep trying until you do.

The End

The woodsman shows you the tunnel that leads to the Cave of Time. You thank him for his help; then, summoning your courage, you crawl through the narrow entrance.

You shiver in the cold damp air as you inch your way along the dark passageway that winds down toward the depths of the Earth. Suddenly you are falling, faster and faster still—falling into a time that has not yet come. It will come, and when it does, your adventure will continue. So it is only for a certain length of time—a few thousand years or so—that this is

The End

Something hits your back with a tremendous thud—the flat side of the Earl of Kent's sword—knocking you to your knees. You are only half conscious as a rope tightly wraps around you, the same rope that, within the hour, will encircle your neck.

The End

You and Michelle follow the trail to the west, which winds around a steep hillside. The sun is about to set when you see a rambling building made of stones and logs. Wildflowers and ferns are growing on the sod-covered roof. Goats and sheep graze nearby.

"This looks as if it was once a monastery," Michelle says, "but someone is using it as a farm." As she speaks, a man walks out of the building.

"Good afternoon, and who are you?" he asks.

"We are travelers from the north," says Michelle, "And who are you?"

"Auguste le Bon," he replies, "late of service to the prince of Lyon, but now I tend this farm for the Philosophers—nobles who have laid down their swords and spend their days mostly in study and contemplation."

Auguste helps you tend to your horses, then takes you inside and gives you bread and cheese and warm broth. While you are eating, he continues, "The Philosopher Knights are at present visiting the court of the prince of Lyon, who, it seems, fear an invasion by King Henry of England. Naturally, the prince has called upon the Philosophers for advice."

"Let us hope Henry does not invade and that peace lies over the land," says Michelle.

"Let us hope so," says Auguste. He asks if

you would like to spend the night, and you and Michelle gratefully accept.

In the morning you ask if he thinks you can safely get past the Dragon of the Ledges.

"I cannot answer that," he says, "for I have never known anyone to try. But I know of a trail through No Man's Forest. It is possible for you to get through it safely, though I don't deny there is a great risk. I will show you the way, if you like. You must leave your horses in our care, however, for whichever route you take, from here on you must travel on foot. The dragon trail is steep and rugged, and the trail through the forest in some places is no more than a tunnel through vines and thorns. Perhaps it would be wiser to wait for the Philosophers to return and to ask their advice."

Michelle beckons you. "What do you think?"

You are tempted to set out on the dragon trail. After all, you are from the twenty-first century, and you know that dragons never really existed. At least you don't think they did.

Go through No Man's Forest, turn to page 18.
Take the dragon trail, turn to page 21.
Wait for the Philosophers to return, turn to page 107.

You run around the side of the tavern, keeping as low as you can so as not to be seen through the basement windows. As you round the corner, you almost crash into a girl with braided brown hair.

"Where are you running to?" she asks, but gives you no time to answer. "I'm Michelle. I live in the tavern. I know you are trying to escape from the English knights. I'll show you where to hide."

You follow her down a flight of stone steps, through a dark passageway, and into a small room filled with casks of wine. The only light comes from cracks at the top of the walls.

"I'll bring you food and milk when it's safe." She turns and hurries up the stairs.

You sit in the cellar, wondering what will become of you and when Michelle will return. You would like to sneak upstairs to get something to eat, but you don't dare.

A few minutes later the door swings open. Michelle steps in, carrying a plate heaped with food.

"Lamb, pears, and fresh bread," she says. "The cook is a friend of mine. I have good news, too. The knights have left. They are looking for you in the woods beyond the bridge." While you eat, you tell Michelle about everything that has happened since you arrived in England through the Cave of Time.

She listens intently. When you finish, she says, "It is a strange story you tell, and I'm not sure I believe you, but I am very glad you have come. My parents died when I was a small child. The innkeeper said I could live at the inn if I swept the floors and helped the cook. Now he works me night and day and hits me if I complain. I have been afraid to run away alone, but we two could go together."

"How?"

"The cook will give us packs of food. I will take blankets and two good horses. There's no moon out tonight, but the stars are bright enough for us. We will ride the road south. There is just one more thing. You cannot expect to hide from anyone in those clothes. They look like a witch must have made them. See what I've brought?" She hands you a small bundle. "Put these on!"

The garments Michelle hands you are rough and don't fit well, but you're glad to get out of your own. Now people won't think you're a devil!

It is almost midnight when Michelle comes to get you. She has the horses ready. In a minute you and she are on horseback, trotting down the road. Along the way, you tell her about the Forbidden Castle and how you think it must be to the south, in the mountains. She agrees to join in your search.

Turn to page 130.

For two days and two nights you and Michelle ride on a road, and then a trail, through pasturelands and forest, stopping only long enough to sleep, eat, and let your horses graze and rest.

On the morning of the third day, you reach a fork in the trail, where you meet a shepherd. "Good morning, friend," you say. "Could you tell us which trail will take us south to the mountains?"

The shepherd looks at you quizzically and shakes his head. "I cannot say, except to say that you cannot go south by going south."

"What new riddle is this?" Michelle demands.

"It is no riddle," the shepherd replies, "but a simple truth, for to the south of us lies No Man's Forest, where the trail is blocked by thickets and thorns, and deadly snakes await travelers. So, if you want to go south, you first must go east or west."

"What lies to the west?" you ask.

The shepherd frowns, and says, "The trail to the west winds through a forest where the Dragon of the Ledges dines on foolish travelers."

"And to the east?" asks Michelle.

"To the east are the lands of the Count Gaston, where half the wolves in Europe roam."

You and Michelle exchange glances.

"We cannot turn back now," she says. "We must go east or west, bad as they both sound."

You go west, turn to page 124.
You go east, turn to page 168.

Life with Garth may not be easy, or even safe, but you prefer the dangers of the forest to those of King Henry's court, and you're confident he will be a good friend.

And so he proves to be. He teaches you to hunt and fish. In the evenings the two of you sit before the fire, and he tells stories of knights and dragons until you fall asleep, dreaming not of knights and dragons but of days gone by with your family and friends, a thousand years in the future.

One day, when the two of you have returned from a hunt, he turns to you and says, "You have grown quick and strong, and wise in the ways of the forest. As for myself, I would rather live in the wilds than in any king's court, but you must choose what sort of life you want to lead. At the western edge of this forest is a road that leads to the castle of Rufus, the mad king of Hereford. Rufus is crazy, but you might find fame and fortune living in his court. I'd rather take my chances with him than with King Henry. He would as soon have you hung as look at you!

"I can give you a password. If you say it three

times to King Rufus's guards, they will admit you to his castle."

Enter the court of Rufus, the mad king of Hereford, turn to page 103.

Continue to live in the forest, turn to page 109.

"I don't think much of Sir Harold's advice," you say. "How about you, Michelle?"

"It sounds ridiculous to me," she says. "I don't believe there is any dragon."

"I'm glad to hear you say that. In the time I come from—the twenty-first century—everyone knows that dragons never lived."

The next morning at sunrise you and Michelle strap on your packs and leave the sleepy Philosophers.

The two of you have been following the dragon trail for half a day when the sky grows darker. You hear thunder.

"Let's hurry, Michelle," you say.

"I'm going as fast as I can," she replies.

The wind blows through the trees. Lightning flashes. You hear a tremendous roar, which rattles your bones.

"That wasn't thunder!" Michelle cries. "It's the dragon!"

Your next thought is: *This can't be happening! Dragons never lived on Earth!*

Unfortunately you never learn more about whether this is so, not knowing whether it was lightning or dragon fire that sizzled you.

The End

You tell Garth of your decision. He wishes you luck, and the next morning you bid him good-bye and set out for the castle. You walk with a light step along the dusty road, cheered by the songs of birds and the smells of the sweet summer air.

By midafternoon you reach a broad, sloping meadow and get your first look at the castle, which is perched on the next hill. Its high stone walls and towers are like a scene from a picture book. A bugle sounds as you approach. A great oak gate swings open, and three knights gallop forth. They rein in their horses beside you. They have some kind of conversation among themselves, then one of them lifts you up onto his horse while another prods you with his sword.

You cling to the saddlehorn as the knights gallop into the castle's courtyard. There they dismount and then turn you over to two guards. The guards drag you down a long flight of crumbling stairs. One of them opens a creaking iron gate. The other shoves you into a dark, musty cell. The door swings shut behind you.

Turn to page 136.

The floor of your quarters is bare rock. On a ledge under a slit in the wall is a pitcher of drinking water and three metal cups. Otherwise the space is bare. There are no windows—only cracks in the walls that provide barely enough light for you to see your cell mate, a thin, sickly looking man whose grimy brown hair hangs halfway to his hips.

"Keep away from me!" he shouts. "Your clothes were made by the devil. . . . Don't come near me!"

"I won't hurt you," you say. "Do you know what they plan to do with me?"

"Most prisoners are beheaded, but in your case, they will burn you at the stake. It's the only way to purge the devil from your soul!"

He steps closer, coughing while he stares at you with pale, watery eyes. "If you are innocent, you won't burn, no matter how hot the fire is!" He laughs, but his laugh turns into a coughing fit. You shrink away, afraid you'll catch a disease.

Two guards peer through the bars. You think they have come for you; instead, they take the man you were talking to. *I won't miss him,* you think.

The guards return about an hour later. You've thought of a couple of questions you might ask.

Ask them to tell you the riddle of the Forbidden Castle, turn to page 41.

Ask what crime you are charged with and whether you'll get a chance to defend yourself, turn to page 143.

Sir Harold gives you and Michelle a sharp knife and a strong, heavy rope, at the end of which you make a noose, and you set out for the dragon trail.

You are happy when, by late afternoon, you come upon a little thatched cottage. Hoping to find a place to stay for the night, you knock on the door. It is opened by a slender woman with long hair. A sparkling green stone hangs from a chain around her neck. You can't stop looking into her glittering eyes.

"You have traveled far," she says. "Come with me and rest. I shall bring you hot broth."

You and Michelle follow her inside. As you start to warm your hands by the fire, the woman bolts the door. Turning toward you, she smiles. It is a strange smile, and she says, "Poor things— you do not seem to be able to tell a witch when you see one. You will learn quite well as I cast my spell."

"What spell?"

"A spell of forgetfulness, so that you will not remember how you returned to your own time . . ."

Turn to page 140.

You are back in your own time. In fact, back in your school library, reading this book. The witch did put a spell of forgetfulness on you. You can't remember how you got back to the Cave of Time. You are just as glad she did, in a way. Instead of catching the dragon with your noose, it's more likely the dragon would have caught you!

What you lived through in medieval Europe seems totally real. Still, you would think that it was just a dream, except for one thing: There's a girl you've never seen at your school, sitting at a table nearby. You would think she was someone who had just transferred, except for one thing: She looks exactly like Michelle. And now she's smiling, hurrying over to speak to you!

The End

"I'll be the Minister of Sanity," you say in a loud, clear voice.

Your statement is met with groans and moans. Some of the lords and ladies begin to cry. Others throw up their hands in protest.

The king stands up, his face is pale. "I only said that as a joke—yet you accept it? This is treason. We have never had a Minister of Sanity, and never will. It would undermine the principles on which our kingdom is founded!"

"We must not have it!" cries the knight sitting near you. "Send this felon from our midst!"

"It's time for a hanging," says another.

"To the stake!" a lady shouts.

"This is insane!" you cry.

"Well, you may be right!" says the king. "But we hereby abolish the position of Minister of Sanity. Henceforth you shall be the Minister of Madness."

To your surprise, everybody cheers.

Bowing, you thank the king and salute the courtiers. "I'll do my best," you say, "to laugh at sadness, cry at smiles, and keep this kingdom free from logic, sense, and all that's wise."

Everyone cheers and claps their hands, even the king. You're not sure if you're already as mad as King Rufus, but you're sure it won't take long.

The End

"What crime am I charged with? Will I get a chance to defend myself?" you ask.

"Do not worry," one of the guards replies. "If you are not in league with the devil, you will go free."

They lead you out into the courtyard. It is filled with knights and ladies, except for a large area in the middle where a pile of wood is neatly stacked.

"How does this trial proceed?" you ask one of the guards.

"It is simple," he says. "They tie you to the stake and light the fire. If you are guilty, you will burn; if you are innocent, you will not be harmed."

You try to run for it, but the guards quickly grab you. They bind your arms to your body with rope. Then, step by step, they march you to the courtyard. The pile of wood has been stacked around a pole in the center. A man in a black robe stands nearby with a rope.

The guards march you toward him. It's not hard to figure out what's going to happen next. There's no way you can keep from going up in smoke.

The End

You knock on the door of Sir Harold, a Philosopher you haven't yet met.

"Come in, come in, come in," he calls impatiently.

When you tell Sir Harold what Sir Charles and Sir René advised you, he shakes his head.

"No, no, no, no, no . . . They're both wrong, for the truth of what a man says does not depend on who he is or who his friends are or on what some prince or archbishop thinks of him. That is a fallacy. Let me tell you what to do: The dragon can be captured by holding a noose outside its cave, because when the dragon comes out, it will walk right into the noose."

"Are you sure that will work?" you ask.

Sir Harold strokes his beard a few times, as if deep in thought, then says, "Yes, yes, yes . . . I'm sure because it is logical and self-evident. Moreover, it stands to reason, and, finally, it is indisputable!"

Decide that Sir Harold's advice is probably as good as any and you might as well follow it, turn to page 138.

Decide that Sir Harold's advice is absurd, turn to page 134.

"I'd like to be the Minister of Guesswork," you say. The assembled lords and ladies murmur their approval.

The king pounds on the table to silence them. "We are glad to hear it," he says. "Since no one can be sure of anything, it takes a wise person to know that all we can do is guess."

The lords and ladies cheer, and again the king pounds on the table. He frowns and wiggles a finger at you.

"We warn you that we expect the highest standards of performance from our ministers. Are you absolutely sure you are capable of serving in this high position?"

You think a moment, then reply, "I guess so."

The lords and ladies murmur their approval.

"Excellent!" says the king. "We guess you will make a fine Minister of Guesswork!"

The Lady in Red and the Minister of Laughter pat you on the back as you begin your dinner. You reflect that if you stay in the mad kingdom, you will soon be as crazy as everyone else. But the roast lamb and the peach pie for dessert are the best you've ever had. You guess Rufus is not as crazy as the kings and knights who spend their lives fighting each other.

The End

"Good afternoon," you say after signaling to the woman to stop. "I've come a long way. Can you tell me where I can find food and shelter for the night?"

She looks you over a moment, then says, "Follow me."

You fall into step next to the cart, wondering where she is going and whether she can really help you. You're not even sure she understood your question.

"Could you tell me what year it is?" you ask.

"Either nine-forty-two or ten-forty-two," the woman says. "I never can remember." You smile to yourself but say nothing. About a mile down the road you reach a small stone house at the edge of the woods. The woman leads you inside and motions for you to sit on a crude oak bench.

"You must wonder who I am," she says in a hoarse voice. "I am called Madame Leeta. I have prophetic powers. I can tell you are a wizard."

"Me? How can you tell that?"

"By your clothes and by your magic object!" She points at the cell phone you're holding. Of course you knew it wouldn't work a thousand years ago! You took it from your pocket out of habit. You realize it must look magical to her!

"You can see into the future better than I can," she continues.

You nod your head, for at that moment you were looking into the future, thinking of your home and family.

Madame Leeta studies you intently. "Since you are a wizard, you can answer the riddle to the Forbidden Castle."

"I have heard of such a riddle, but don't know what it is."

She leans closer to you, and in a soft, hoarse voice, she says:

> "Somewhere south, where it's colder,
> Where that which falls stays where it is,
> You'll find what isn't what it is."

She leans even closer and clutches your arm. "Baron de Sal has promised me twenty gold pieces if I can find the Forbidden Castle. He thinks I can solve the riddle. And I can! But I need your help!"

"I'll have to think about it," you say. "Do you have any idea where this castle is?"

"Ah!" she exclaims. "You are a clever wizard, not letting me know how much you know. To find the Forbidden Castle, you have to solve the riddle. And to solve the riddle, you have to find the Forbidden Castle. Heh, heh." She stares at you with glittering eyes. "Stay at my cottage tonight. I will feed you lamb stew, butter bread, and fresh berries and cakes. Tomorrow we shall combine our powers and find the castle. The baron will take us there."

You need a good meal and a place to stay, but it's hard to believe that Madame Leeta can help you solve the riddle or find the castle. Having now had a glimpse of the world as it was almost a thousand years ago, you're thinking you'd be happier back in your own time. Maybe you should forget about the Forbidden Castle and look for an entrance to the Cave of Time near the field where you arrived.

Team up with Madame Leeta in search of the castle,
turn to page 112.
Try to find your way to your own time, turn to page 99.

Sir Charles gives you directions through the forest to the estate of the Count de Rue. Early the next morning you and Michelle pack as much food and supplies as you can carry, and set out on your way.

For two days you follow first one trail, then another, through woods so dense that you almost never see the sun. The farther you walk, the more you realize that Sir Charles's directions make no sense. You are forced to admit to each other that you are lost.

You wander on, hoping to find your way, but the trails you follow are like passageways in an endless maze. Neither you or Michelle are ever seen again.

The End

You look the king in the eye and try to sound as if you know what you're talking about.

"This has to do with the setting sun," you say. "The sun falls but actually stays where it is."

King Henry replies, "What do you mean it stays where it is? Anyone can see that the sun doesn't stay where it is. It falls below the horizon!"

"But it does stay where it is, Your Majesty. The sun seems to fall below the horizon when it sets, because the Earth is turning, but the sun itself stays where it is!"

"What do you mean, the Earth is turning?" The king jabs his finger at you. "Are you trying to make a fool of me? What you speak is heresy. Anyone can see that the Earth does not turn. The sun travels around the Earth every day and falls at night!"

If only you could show the king he is wrong, but he gives a command to the guards, and they order you to march ahead of them, down the steps leading to the dungeon.

You take out the magic crystal the witch gave you, but before you can say the magic word, a guard whacks it out of your hand and out of reach forever.

The End

It's slow going through the thick pine forest, and you're afraid you'll not be out of it before dark. But late in the day you come out onto open land. You are glad to see a broad stream up ahead and rolling fields beyond it.

"I think we have reached the lands of Count Gaston," says Michelle. No sooner has she spoken than you hear the howling of a wolf in the distance; then another—closer. Then another!

"They are on our scent," says Michelle. "It will not be long before they find us."

As she talks, you look for something to use as a weapon. You pick up a fallen branch and break it in two. Now you have a good club. You can probably defend yourself against a single wolf, but you hear others, much closer! The pack is closing in.

Michelle points to a tall pine with branches reaching almost to the ground. "Quick! We could climb up into that tree."

You had the same thought, but another idea occurs to you: If you could walk through the stream for a ways, the wolves would lose your scent.

Run to the tree and climb it, turn to page 111.

Tell Michelle to follow you and run for the stream, turn to page 97.

"Okay," you say. "Get over to the left of the rat, and I'll come up behind it with my pack."

You both get in position. Michelle blows the horn and keeps blowing. It makes a very loud, unpleasant sound. The rat freezes, eyes on Michelle. You bring your pack down on it and scoop it up, then fold over the top of your pack so the rat can't get out. It's all you can do not to let go as it struggles to get free.

"Nice work!" Michelle says. "Now what will we do with it?"

At that moment the guard opens the gate. "What was that noise?" he demands. "It sounded like a horn." Seeing the horn, he tries to snatch it from Michelle, who backs off, leading him on, so that you and she are closer to the door than the guard is. You see a chance to escape. But you first need to distract the guard.

Hold the pack up to the guard and say "Take this!"
turn to page 155.

Yell at Michelle, "Throw the horn into the corner!"
turn to page 156.

"No," you say, "I'll stand over in the corner and blow the horn, and you catch it in your satchel. Just do it!"

"All right," Michelle says reluctantly. The two of you get in position. You blow the horn. The rat freezes and looks at the horn as if hypnotized by the strange sound. Michelle brings the satchel down on the rat, but somehow doesn't get the opening sealed. The rat jumps free and comes at you. You blow your horn again, hoping to stop it. But it keeps coming.

Try to kick it, turn to page 161.
Try to hit it with the horn, turn to page 162.

"Here, take this instead!" You hold the pack to the guard, inviting him to see what's inside. He leans over to get a look. You pull back the cover. The rat jumps at the guard's face. He screams. Michelle hits him over the head with the horn, breaking it in two.

The guard is still reeling while you and Michelle escape through the door. You run up the stairs, then down a long dark hall. There's light at the end—it leads to the courtyard.

Turn to page 159.

"Michelle, throw the horn into the corner," you cry. She does just that. The guard goes to grab it, and Michelle and you are out the door.

You swing the gate shut and lock in the guard. Then, still holding your pack with the rat in it, you run up the stairs with Michelle right behind you. You can hear the guard screaming at you from the locked cell.

"Quick," Michelle says. "Follow me!" She turns down a passageway you hadn't noticed, then out through a window onto the rampart, then to the great iron gate at the entrance to the castle.

The gate is open, but there's a guard on each side. By this time you're ahead of Michelle. You run up to the guard.

"Look here—the crown jewels," you say, and shove your pack in front of his nose. He grabs it, opens it, and screams as the rat jumps in his face. By this time you and Michelle are both through the gate. Looking back, you see that the guard you fooled is bleeding from the nose, still screaming in horror from what happened to him. The other guard is chasing you, his saber drawn.

Michelle hasn't looked back. She's kept

running, and it's you the guard catches up to, dropping you to the ground with a terrible blow. You realize it's all over for you—you only hope that Michelle gets away.

The End

You throw down your knife and surrender. The guards bring you before the prince and tell him how you got away from your cell and stole a knife.

The prince smiles when he hears this. "Here is a youth with spirit and daring," he says. "Just what I need in my court!"

To your amazement the prince sees that you have a private chamber and new clothes. Later, he summons you before him.

"I could tell you are not an ordinary person," he says. "You might be able to help me with something. I'm trying to solve a riddle."

"Is it about the Forbidden Castle?" you ask.

The prince's face lights up.

"Yes, how did you know? You must be a wizard." He looks at you curiously, then says, "I'm sure you can solve the riddle and find the castle."

Can you? You decide to try, and if you don't succeed, find your way back to the Cave of Time and start over.

The End

You run out to the courtyard, or what's more like a barnyard. Chickens are scurrying around. A rooster looks at you and crows. A wagon loaded with hay is nearby. You climb in and hide under the hay. An hour goes by, then another—at least it might be another. You can't be sure, because you've fallen asleep. When you wake up you're not in the wagon anymore, but in the hut of a peasant.

"You must be hungry," he says as you sleepily sit up.

"How did I get here?" you ask.

"In the wagon you were sleeping in," he says. "It was quite a surprise to find you when I unloaded my hay. Do you want me to take you back to the castle?"

"No!"

"I didn't think so. Well, you'll be safe here. My wife and I have plenty of work for you to do, but you can be sure we will be kind to you. We have no child of our own. So finding you under the hay was like finding a gift."

"It was a gift to me as well," you say. "If it were not for you, I'd be back in the dungeon by now, or maybe not even alive!"

The End

You throw your knife ahead so you can pick it up after you land. Then you take a deep breath and jump. You're hoping to land squarely and tumble forward, but you are slightly off balance. The soft grass gives way as you land, and your weight comes down on one side of your ankle.

You lie beneath the castle wall. You don't think any bones are broken, but your ankle is so badly sprained that you can hardly walk. The guards have no trouble catching you. No use using the witch's crystal. It won't heal your ankle, and if you put a spell on these guards, others will overwhelm you. Soon you are back in the dungeon again, and you have not just one rat for company again, but a dozen of them!

The End

You aim a swift kick at the rat, but it evades your foot, and in an instant you feel its needlelike teeth piercing your ankle. You scream, and wake up, realizing you've had a nightmare! What a relief! But it's not a relief! You're not in your own bed at home. You're not even in the twenty-first century. You're in a pile of hay in a dungeon in Spain six hundred years ago. Michelle is not here, nor is a rat or a goat horn. You hear footsteps. A guard is coming. Some new frightening adventure is about to begin.

The End

You try to hit the rat with the horn, miss it, and break the horn. The rat scurries off to the side. At least it didn't bite you.

A guard has come and is looking through the bars. "What was that noise? It sounded like a horn! There it is. You broke it, you fool!"

Michelle is huddled in a corner, eyeing the rat.

You've never felt so bad in your life. You might as well give up hope of finding the Forbidden Castle. Unless . . . unless—you're in the Forbidden Castle!

The End

You run as fast as you can to the bridge. As you get near it, you look back toward the tavern. The driver must have woken up and sounded the alarm: The Earl of Kent and his knights are galloping toward you, with swords already drawn!

Starting across the bridge, you hear the horses close behind you. If you can just get to the end of the bridge, you can run into the woods. But will you even get that far?

Try to make it across the bridge and into the woods, turn to page 165.

Jump off the bridge and into the river, turn to page 164.

You vault over the bridge's railing and jump. The river is fed by melting snow from the mountains, and you feel an icy numbness as you splash below the surface. You struggle to keep your head above water, gasping for air as the current carries you downstream.

You set out for the riverbank, but the swirling water pulls you from shore. The current forces you against the sharp edge of a boulder, opening a gash in your leg. It hardly hurts—you're so numb with cold. Your strength is failing, but you keep swimming, knowing that the farther you can get downstream, the farther you'll be from your pursuers.

You are barely conscious when the current sweeps you against a fallen tree. The water is calmer. You work your way along the tree trunk to shore and crawl up the steep muddy slope. As you reach the tall grass along the bank, you flop quietly, too exhausted to move. Your leg is still bleeding. It's beginning to hurt. You're so exhausted and bruised that you hardly care that you're still alive.

Night is coming on. There is no chance King Henry's knights will find you. And no chance you'll survive until dawn.

The End

You hear the galloping horses thumping on the wooden planks, and you run even faster, getting almost to the end of the bridge.

Turn to page 123.

The chancellor orders the guards to untie you. He leads you out of the courtyard and through an archway, beyond which is a heavy oak door guarded by two men with swords. One of them opens the door. The chancellor pushes you into a waiting room, where three guards stand over you. After a few minutes he returns and leads you into a large octagonal room lighted by rows of casement windows over the rough stone walls. At the far end of a long oak table sits King Henry himself, a tall, thin young man with a long pointed beard. A gold-leaf crown sits slightly tilted on his head.

The king looks at you curiously a moment, then he says, "We have never been so happy as when we learned that you know the solution to the riddle. Tell us what it is!"

You have been trying desperately to think of a solution. You think of the first line of the riddle: "Somewhere south, where it's colder . . ." At least you have a couple of ideas.

Normally it will be warmer, not cooler, if you go south. Mountains might be cooler, even though they are farther south, and, of course, the coldest place of all is the South Pole!

"Well?" The king leans forward impatiently.

Say "The Forbidden Castle is to the south, but high in the
mountains, where it's colder," turn to page 86.

Say "The Forbidden Castle is to the south, on the way to
the South Pole," turn to page 93.

You and Michelle ride east, through forests and meadows, over hills, through valleys, and across brooks and streams. It's well past midday when you unsaddle your horses and sit in the shade of a towering elm tree to rest and eat.

You are about to resume your journey when two men approach on foot. They are dressed in peasant clothes, though one of them wears a gold medallion on his chest.

"Good afternoon," you say. "I wonder if you could tell us how far we are from the southern mountains?"

"The mountains are only a day's journey, but you'll have to cross the lands of Count Gaston," replies one of the men. "You will find the trails so steep that you won't be able to use your horses, but we shall take care of them for you."

"What do you mean?" Michelle cries.

Suddenly, the men untether your horses! "I said we will take care of them."

"What are you doing?" you shout.

"We're doing you a favor," says the other man.

You get out your crystal. If there was ever a time to cast a spell, this is it!

You hold up the crystal and say the magic word. The two men freeze. You stare at them, amazed—they look like realistic statues.

"Let's get out of here," Michelle says. "We don't know how long the spell will last."

You realize she's right. In a few seconds you're on your horses. You ride off at a good pace. Looking back, you see that the men are still motionless, though you have a feeling the spell will wear off soon.

Turn to page 170.

You've been riding for an hour along a well-marked trail, but now, ahead of you, lies a dense pine forest. The trail continues into the forest, but the horses balk. It's too narrow for them between the thickly packed trees.

"Quelle ironie," says Michelle, forgetting for a moment you can't understand French. You don't have to in this case because it's obvious she's thinking the same thing you are: You can't continue on the trail with the horses. From here on you'll have to proceed on foot. Fortunately, you find a farm nearby. You arrange to leave your horses there until you return for them. It's midafternoon by the time you get back to where the trail enters the forest.

Turn to page 151.

"We have come this far," you whisper to Michelle. "I'm not going to turn back now."

As quietly as you can, you pick your way through the bleached white bones, hoping the dragon will not hear you. Michelle follows close behind.

The hissing grows louder. Sparks, glowing cinders, and billowing puffs of smoke fill the air. Looking down, you see the empty eye sockets of a human skull staring up at you. Gritting your teeth, you continue past the rock.

The smell of smoke gets stronger. You pass some tall pine trees, and now can see before you a fire of blazing boughs. Sitting beside it is an old man with a white beard. He holds a blacksmith's bellows to the flames and blows fire and sparks toward you. You jump back in time to avoid being singed by the leaping flames. He seems too busy to notice you as he lifts a ram's horn to his mouth and blows an eerie, wailing blast— the terrible sound of the Dragon of the Ledges! Michelle runs up, laughing.

The old man lays down his bellows and his horn. He stands there—hands outstretched. "You have met the dragon," he says. "You are the first who dared come so close!"

"Ah-ha!" says Michelle. "Wait until the prince of Lyon learns your secret!"

"He already knows my secret. He ordered me to stay here and keep the people from finding the Forbidden Castle."

"That's what we're looking for!" you say.

The old man looks wistfully upward for a moment. "'Where that which falls stays where it is . . . ,'" he says, smiling.

"Yes. That's part of the riddle!"

"Then follow me."

The old man leads you farther along a winding trail and up over a high ridge. Standing on the trail, blocking your way, is a very large lion.

Once you get over the shock, your brain begins to work again. "I can't believe there is a lion here in the mountains of Europe," you say.

"It is not a lion as you know it," the old man says. "It is a magic lion. If you try to get past it, it will devour you. But if you say the secret name, it will stand aside and let you pass."

Say the secret name is "Oddysus," turn to page 51.
Say the secret name is "Odysseus," turn to page 175.

"Don't worry," you say. "I'll solve the riddle soon."

"How soon?" the baron demands, his voice rising.

"Very soon," you say. "Now let's keep moving."

The baron grumbles, but you pay no attention to him as you lead him and Madame Leeta higher and higher up the mountain road. If you can only get near the top of the mountain, you'll be able to see a great distance in all directions. Maybe you'll see the Forbidden Castle.

But climbing becomes increasingly difficult. The road has narrowed; only a rough trail lies ahead. The baron has to leave his horses and carriage in the care of a shepherd. From then on you all continue on foot, and you can only go half a mile or so before the way becomes too steep to climb. You'll be in big trouble if you can't see the castle once you reach the next ridge.

Turn to page 52.

You say, "Odysseus." The lion steps aside and lies down. You hear a noise like a small electric motor: It's the lion, purring like a cat!

Sure that it's now safe to go on, you and Michelle walk past the lion and continue on the trail, up a ridge. As you reach the top of the ridge, you hear a rushing sound. *Is it the wind, or is it the water?* you wonder.

"Follow me," you say to Michelle, and you start walking toward the sound. Following the steep, curving mountain path, you come to a clearing, from which you can see in the distance a great waterfall, and beyond it, the gleaming white walls and four ivory towers of a castle! Could this be the Forbidden Castle you've been looking for?

The second part of the riddle comes to your mind.

"Michelle, the castle we're looking at is by a waterfall! It's where what falls stays where it is!"

"You may be right," says Michelle. "A waterfall does fall but stays where it is, but what about the third line of the riddle, about the castle itself? It isn't what it is. How can this be?"

"I don't know, but maybe we can find out."

You follow a trail that descends into a ravine

that is steep and rugged, and you are glad to reach the bottom safely and begin the long climb up the mountainside. When you finally reach the ledge and look straight into the silvery cascade, the waterfall sounds like music in your ears. The pines and ferns glisten with spray. You work your way around to the left of the falls and climb to a higher ledge.

Now what you have been looking for is right in front of you. Gleaming in the late afternoon sunlight are walls built upon walls—massive blocks of chalk-white stones, and, soaring above them, four gold-capped ivory towers that seem to pierce the mountain sky. The Forbidden Castle!

"Never have I seen anything so beautiful!" Michelle says.

Looking down toward the valley below, you see a line of mounted horses. At least a hundred men are following on foot.

"Michelle, it's King Henry and his army! His wise men must have solved the riddle."

"Do you think he can conquer the Forbidden Castle?" she asks.

"I don't know," you answer, and hurry up the slope toward the castle. Strange to see, the drawbridge lies open. There aren't even chains or ropes by which it could be raised. As you get close, a tiny woman wearing a long, gray cloak comes forth to greet you.

"Welcome!" she calls to you. "I am Sister Anna."

"Good afternoon, Sister," you say. "Where is the prince who rules this great castle?"

"And why is it called the Forbidden Castle?" Michelle adds.

Sister Anna smiles. "There is no prince or knights here—only the Sisters of Hope. You see, once a great prince ruled this castle, attended by a splendid court, but a plague swept across the lands and killed all the lords and ladies who lived here—everyone!

"For years no one dared to come near, so it became known as the Forbidden Castle. But we Sisters of Hope vowed not to be afraid of plagues, whether borne by rats or kings or knaves. We came to tend the sick and helpless. Since then, good fortune has come to all who visit here in friendship."

As Sister Anna is speaking, the third line of the riddle comes to your mind: "You'll find what isn't what it is."

"Is this a castle, or isn't it?" you ask.

The sister smiles. "You need only look at it to see that it is a castle," she says. "And yet it is not a castle with a lord and his vassals. It is a convent and a refuge for the poor and the helpless."

So you think: *It isn't what it is!*

You have been so amazed by the sister's story that you have forgotten about King Henry and his army. But now you hear bugles blowing, shouts, and the sound of horses! Other sisters come forth from the castle. You and Michelle step aside as they form a line to face King Henry and his powerful army, which is now approaching.

You watch anxiously as the armored troops come to a halt. King Henry dismounts. He walks up to Sister Anna, draws his sword, and holds it high above his head. The sisters stand motionless before him. The king hurls his sword to the ground.

"How can I conquer a castle defended by little old ladies?" he says. "It would violate the code of chivalry!"

Sister Anna steps forward and touches his arm. "And pray, great king," she says, "how would it profit you to conquer this castle? You already have a castle of your own. Were you to rule all of Europe, I am sure you would soon have more problems than pleasures. So stay if you wish; drink our nectar and eat honey bread. Forget about conquests, and go in peace."

The king stares at the castle and at the mountains and the waterfall. He slowly shakes his head.

"What will I tell my knights?" he murmurs. "They will laugh at me for leading them here!"

"Tell them," Sister Anna says with a smile, "that you led them here to teach them a lesson."

King Henry turns toward his followers. You can't hear the exact words, but you know that he is telling them the lesson he's learned, and that conquering all of Europe is no longer his goal.

Turn to page 182.

The Sisters of Hope invite you and Michelle to stay with them as long as you'd like. During the days that follow they tell you wonderful stories of kings and knights and dragons.

You learn to weave tapestries, which will be sold to raise money to help the poor. Each day, when your work is done, you ride the mountain ponies, ski on the snowy slopes, and swim in the sparkling pools beneath the waterfall, all heated by hot springs and as warm as you could wish for.

Michelle is completely happy and has decided to become one of the Sisters of Hope herself. You don't feel the same way. As good as life is here, you spend more and more time thinking of home.

"What is troubling you?" Sister Anna asks one day.

"I dream of finding the entrance to the Cave of Time so that I can return to my home in the twenty-first century."

"It need not be a dream," she says, and hands you a tiny wooden pipe. "If you blow on this pipe, it will summon a unicorn. You need only follow it, and it will lead you to the Cave of Time."

Your eyes open wide. "I thought unicorns never existed."

"Oh, but they do," she replies, "though it will be difficult to believe that when you return to your own time. You may not even believe you visited the Forbidden Castle. Yet, you will never forget it."

Just as Sister Anna promised, a unicorn leads you to an entrance to the Cave of Time, and you find your way back to your own time and home and family. All that remains of your journey is your memory of the Forbidden Castle, and a tiny wooden pipe. And though it makes a pretty sound, no unicorn has come. Not so far.

The End